IS ANYBODY THERE?

Joanne turned to stare at the hall mirror and saw again her mother standing there. Hair so beautifully coiffed, dyed, of course; make-up hiding her skin, her body shaped by diet, exercise, and a one-piece girdle and bra, her hands hidden by white gloves, her legs sheathed in flesh-colored nylon. Even her eyes were covered, by contact lenses.

For a terrifying moment Joanne wondered if there was anything behind all the layers. Would it be like stripping away the bandages of the invisible man, revealing only air beneath? She touched her own face, then pinched her leg until it hurt.

"I am real," she said softly. "I know I am real." The fear persisted and she knew it was because she doubted. How could she be real, if her mother wasn't? Why should she be real? Nobody else was. Nobody at all.

Two brilliant novellas of mounting terror and suspense by one of today's most acclaimed writers of science fiction, Kate Wilhelm.

Abyss

Two Novellas
by
Kate Wilhelm

A NATIONAL GENERAL COMPANY

ABYSS

*A Bantam Book / published by arrangement with
Doubleday & Company, Inc.*

PRINTING HISTORY
Mercury Press edition published 1967
Doubleday edition published 1971
Bantam edition published November 1973

Contents

The Plastic Abyss

DOROTHY PAUSED AT THE DOOR TO THE LIVING ROOM and listened for a moment. Her husband was talking, his voice insistent, not raised, never, ever raised, but inescapable. She deliberately didn't hear the words, listened instead to the tone, the quality of his voice that now made his words sound so much more meaningful than they had been when he had practiced on her in halting phrases, stumbling over his ideas, garbling them. She was the yellow pulp paper on which he tried out his first draft; the guests who listened soberly were fine, smooth, twenty-pound bond. She turned from the door, to go back to the patio where she had retreated several minutes earlier. No one expected her to rejoin them that night, although no one would object if she did; they all liked Gary's pretty, young wife. She sat down and looked past the pool out over the sand to the ocean shimmering under a gibbous moon.

After a few moments she knew that she couldn't sit still any longer and she walked outside, kicked off her sandals, and went down to the hard sand of the high-tide mark and watched the play of waves. The sand

1

felt cool to her bare feet, the wind cool on her cheeks. She wished that she had stopped to put on her bathing suit, or shorts; the wind was whipping her skirt about her legs. The light from the moon caught on the advancing front of the waves, creating gleaming yellow and black walls. The waves broke and the light shattered into thousands, millions of pieces, fractured, lost. And new walls formed. Farther out there was a broad undulating avenue of gold that stretched forever.

The walls advanced, broke, shattered. She started to stroll along the edge of the water. The golden avenue moved with her, inviting her to walk away. She thought of the talk going on in her house: Gary insistent, driving; Mr. Rosenthal, head of the legal department, listening inscrutably; Dr. Jarvis, a Ph.D. psychologist who was the public relations department, listening with his eyes half closed, doodling but making notes from the doodles that later he would be able to decipher. The other three men also listening raptly, taking their cue from Rosenthal and Jarvis. Gary talking: "Gentlemen, think of what I am saying. This material can absorb eighty-five per cent of all the radiant energy that strikes it. Absorb it and turn it into electricity to be stored in self-contained batteries —starlight, sunlight, moonlight, artificial light, radio waves. You name it. With the additional research that a government contract will make possible, we hope to increase that capacity to plus ninety per cent." But more polished, smoother. That was the first draft.

"Wouldn't that create an abyss?" she had asked, during dress rehearsal.

"Could. But, we can project whatever we want, and that's what will be seen."

"Illusion, then. Another shade of reality."

"Don't go mystical on me, Dorothy. Reality doesn't come in shades or gradations. It is real or it isn't. This table is real. This house. You. I. A projected image is a real image. It's just the damn semantics that makes that statement sound contradictory."

She touched the table as he had, a pale polished table with curved legs, on heavy glass rug protectors. The rug beneath it was pale blue, deeply carved, inches thick. She slid her foot on the rug.

"Honey, what's wrong?" Gary was watching her intently.

"Nothing. Nothing. Sometimes none of this seems real, or if it is, then I can't be. I don't know."

He took her hands, laughing, and pulled her to her feet. She was tall, they were well matched. She hardly tilted her head at all for his kiss. When the kiss was over, her heart was beating harder, and she could feel the pulse in her throat, and the heat on her cheeks flushing them. He looked at her, still smiling. "Real?"

She nodded, and arm in arm they walked through the living room, into a hall, into the bedroom. Their love-making was hard, intense, almost desperate, she thought later when it was over, and she was almost asleep in his arms, drifting, wondering why he was so desperate about making love to her, wondering why, when she closed her eyes, the house was so hard to believe in, wondering why, when Gary was away, he became less real to her. She should go back to work, back to writing articles, to traveling, prying, learning. Vegetating luxuriously was not good for her. Old man Davenport would be happy if she expressed an interest in writing the biography of his grandfather, or even an article about his attempts to clear the name of his grandfather. She could move her things to one of the spare bedrooms, make an office there, repaint it, haul out Vickie's furniture. . . . Not Vickie's, Gary's. He had selected everything for the house, hired the decorator and made all the arrangements. Not Vickie's things. But it felt like Vickie's house. She stirred restlessly, but settled down again almost immediately without waking up more than she was already. In her near dream state she could see the guest room outfitted as an office: steel blue walls, cold blue, with silver in the drapes, straight lines, hard surfaces where thoughts bounced, gathered strength, didn't suffocate in plush softness.

She still recalled the dream image vividly. Was it a real image, projected into her consciousness from . . . where? It seemed more real than the fairy-tale house with its women's magazine interior.

The walls of moonlight advanced and broke up into millions of pieces and each gleaming bit was lost. Like a phoenix a new wall grew, solid, glowing with light. She was in a strange city where all the buildings were polished marble, windowless as high as she could see, unbroken, green shading to black with specks of gold and silver. In both directions the broad, empty street vanished in solid darkness. The walls formed a broad upright avenue with a strip of light above them, but even as she noticed the light of the sky, it faded and darkened and there were only the walls. She walked, touching the wall on her left, letting her hand run along its smooth surface. It was cool, smooth as glass. Soon there would be a doorway, an arch, or a mall with windows and showcases. She moved soundlessly in a silent world, and she came to the corner and turned, keeping her hand on the wall. The corner was sharp, unequivocal. Soon now there would be a door, a section of show windows. Why was no one else about? She could hear only her own breathing and, looking down, realized that she was being so quiet because she had no shoes on. The sidewalk was twenty feet wide here, then the street at least twice that width, another sidewalk, another wall, faceless and unbroken. Another corner. She was content to walk, thinking. If you stare into the abyss long enough, the abyss stares back. Nietzsche? But if they were projecting images on top of the abyss, could you see if anything stared back? Or would it be a one-way view? No gradations in reality. Everything out there is a projection; only I am real. Whose projection?

A long wall, green shading to black, flecked with silver and gold, sometimes the silver and gold predominating, sometimes not. Unbroken, smooth, hard, cool. An abrupt figure-ground shift, and the walls were now horizontal, with broad golden avenues radiating from a center that was distant, that became the vanishing point. A change in her direction to step onto the golden avenue.

"Hi!"

She stopped, ankle deep in water that chilled her legs as the waves broke in their rush to land, sending spray to her knees. She turned and looked about wildly, not knowing where she was, or who had spoken. Then she saw a figure, a man. The moonlight was too dim now to see more than that, a man, a figure.

She left the water and looked up and down the beach uncertainly. She couldn't recognize any of it.

"Cigarette?" The man came toward her holding out a pack. She took one and he struck a match for her, cupping it with both hands until she had a light, shielding the flame, also concealing his face while examining hers.

"Thanks," she said, and started to move away, turning around, the water to her right. The man fell into step beside her, not talking. They walked side by side until her cigarette was gone, then she said, "Do you live around here?"

"Yes. You?"

"Right down there," she said, pointing generally down the beach. She still didn't know how far she had walked. She wanted to add, with my husband, but didn't. He wasn't being pushy, or even friendly, really. It was rather as if they both happened to be going in the same direction and it would have been more awkward to walk with beach separating them than it was to walk side by side. Then she saw the DePuys' house and involuntarily she sighed her relief. Along with her relief came a feeling of shocked surprise. This was at least a mile from her house. What had possessed her to walk so far? She felt as if she must have been sleep-walking, and the whole thing was vague and dream-like. She could remember no thoughts that had pre-occupied her, nothing.

When they got within sight of her house, the strange man stopped. "So long, Mrs. Hazlett."

Dorothy felt a touch of surprise. He knew her? She tried to see his face again, but there was too little light. "Good-by," she said. As she walked on she had the feeling that he was still standing there, watching her. She didn't turn around to see. At the walk that marked her yard, she did look, but the white sand stretched in both directions unbroken, uninhabited. She continued to the arched entrance of the garden, stopped for her sandals, and headed for the outside shower to clean the sand from her feet. She was thinking what a curious encounter it had been with the man on the beach, wondering who he was, how he happened to know her name and house. Off to her right, hidden by a shadow-like oleander with pale blossoms floating about it, was the swimming pool and clusters of patio furniture. She heard a clink of ice against glass and she paused with her hand on the shower faucet. Gary and his guests out for a late swim?

"Will Davenport make a patent application for this new development?"

"If Hazlett gets his way."

"Stall things awhile. Give me time to get in touch with Brock. I'll get back to you in a couple of days."

They moved away and there was a splash from the pool. Dorothy hadn't recognized either of the voices. She didn't turn on the water after all, but went around the house and entered her bedroom suite through a French window. The house was cold. She adjusted the air-conditioner and showered, and then paced, waiting for Gary to return.

Gary came in with his terry robe across his shoulders. He grinned at Dorothy and tossed his robe to a chair and began to undo his belt on the brief bathing suit, exposing a strip of white skin.

"Did we wake you up?"

"I wasn't asleep yet. Gary, who is Brock? I heard two of those men talking about a Brock. . . ."

He was paying no attention to her. He stripped off his trunks and, carrying them, started to the shower. Only the narrow band that his trunks covered was pale, everywhere else he was suntanned to a deep red-brown, an Indian color. Every morning he swam a mile, then trotted back along the beach that same mile. His eyes were like pale milk chocolate, and his hair was bleached out almost blond. "Nice party," he said. "I think Jarvis is completely sold, and that means a lot at this point. He'll swing old man Davenport to our side."

"Gary? Do you know anyone named Brock?"

He paused in the doorway to the bathroom. "Brock? Don't think so. Why?"

"I told you. I heard two of your guests talking. One said to stall you until he gets in touch with Brock. . . ."

Gary shrugged and turned from her to enter the bathroom. Dorothy followed him. "It sounded like a conspiracy or something."

Gary stopped and turned once more, smiling gently at her. "Honey, you were dreaming. How could you have heard anyone talking? It was a dream."

She shook her head. "I wasn't in bed yet. I was coming back from a walk on the beach. On the other side of the bushes by the pool I could hear them talking. One said that the other one should stall until he got in touch with Brock. The other one said all right, or something, and they both moved away toward the pool. I heard them clearly."

Gary touched her cheek lightly and shook his head. "Baby, I came in to see if you wanted to take a dip with us. You were asleep. You must have heard me moving about, getting my suit on. It started you dreaming."

"For heaven's sake, Gary, I should know if I was in bed asleep or not. I heard them!"

"Okay. We'll talk about it in the morning." He stepped into the shower and pulled the sliding doors shut.

Dorothy turned furiously back to the bedroom and stopped. The bed was mussed, her pillow indented, the top sheet thrown back diagonally across the bed, like a streamer of blue flowers against a paler blue bottom sheet. Her slippers were there, one on its side, the other straight, the way she usually left them. The book she had been reading that week was on the table, along with her cigarettes and lighter, cigarette stubs in the ashtray. Behind her was a pounding like a waterfall in the shower, but when she moved a step farther from the door, she moved into a profound silence, and all she could see was the ashtray with cigarette stubs, all she could hear was the ticking of the slender clock that was on the table, with silver hands now indicating three-fifteen. After three? Impossible. She had left the living room before twelve.

Angrily she shook her head and sat down at the dressing table and brushed her hair hard. When Gary emerged from the shower, toweling himself, she said, "Okay, joke's over. This is a side you've kept pretty well hidden, you know. Practical jokes at three in the morning somehow just don't seem all that funny." She stared at him in the mirror and pulled the brush; electricity from her hair crackled in the silence that followed. Gary's face showed surprise, then bewilderment, and finally resignation. He shrugged and pulled back the bedspread from the second bed. Dorothy continued to watch his reflection. "Why did you do that?" She pointed to her bed. "When did you do it?"

"Honey, let's go to sleep now. We'll talk about it in the morning."

He rolled over. Dorothy lay awake until dawn when the heavy drapes gave the early light a dusky, used look. She fell asleep to dream of herself trying to peer around a corner where she knew she would find another version of the same girl, also trying to peer around the corner, from the other direction.

She woke up when Gary did, but she didn't get up, or speak to him. She kept her eyes closed and listened to his movements about the bedroom, in the dressing room, the bathroom, back to the bedroom. He stopped at the hall door, and for a moment she thought he would say something to her, but then he left, and soon afterward she heard the car start, crunch on the pebble driveway, and fade away. A gull screeched.

The men were due for lunch with old Mr. Davenport at twelve-thirty, and sometime after four Gary would be back alone. She resolved never to bring up his stupid practical joke again, or to mention Brock, or the conspiratorial exchange, anything from the night before.

Gary was in a black mood when he returned. "Davenport is cracking up, the old bastard," he said, mixing a martini. "He doesn't give a damn about this new idea. All he has on his mind now is that goddam celebration he's so hot about. For chrissake why's it so important to him to prove his grandfather was innocent? Who gives a damn?"

"That's only half of it," Dorothy said. "The half he understands and talks about. The other reasons, the ones he can't even put into words, are more to the point. He has to reenact the past to make it real. It's disconnected now, and things have to be tied together or we forget them. How can something be real if it isn't remembered? So by making it live again, even by proxy, the past will be realer, his place in the present will be firmer. There has to be a feeling of continuity."

"Good God," Gary said. "The old man wants his family name cleared. It's as simple as that. Pride. Just don't go profound on me right now. Okay?"

"This sort of mysticism is as simple as the mind of the most childish ancestor worshiper. It isn't especially profound. This is one of the ways we have of knowing our own reality. Through our parents, and their parents." Deliberately Dorothy goaded him, still angry with him for the not-so-funny joke and his refusal to admit to it. She knew he didn't want her to talk, she was supposed to listen to him, or, at best, to talk about what he wanted to hear. She realized with surprise how her own interests had dwindled and dropped away since their marriage.

"That's drivel, and you know it."

"No. It really isn't. We keep heirlooms, other people's if not our own. Antiques. Name our children for grandparents. Erect elaborate cenotaphs. . . ."

"To prove we're real?"

"Yes."

"Honey, just shut up. Right?" She grinned, but he was not amused, didn't even notice. "The old man's cracked on this subject. Okay, so we go along with him, play it his way. On Tuesday he wants us to have dinner with him and meet the reincarnation of his grandfather." Gary slammed his fist on the bar in frustration. He stared at his clenched fist for a moment, then relaxed it. "We don't have anything lined up for the weekend, do we, anything we can't get out of?"

"Joanne's coming. You promised her that you'd go sailing with her this time. That's all."

He shrugged it off. Joanne was his seventeen-year-old daughter. She lived with his first wife in Atlanta. "You and Jo can take the boat out. She doesn't need me. Okay?" Taking his drink with him, he started for the door. "I'll be back in a few minutes. A couple of calls to make."

They both knew that Joanne wouldn't go sailing with Dorothy, that she would sulk the entire weekend if he broke his promise again, but they pretended that it would be all right. Dorothy poured a second cup of coffee for herself and wandered to the patio while Gary made telephone calls, and when he joined her there, it was dark. She could only guess from the tone of his voice that his plans were not going well.

Softly she said, "Why do you have to push so hard, Gary? It isn't your discovery, your company. You just work for Davenport. Why does it mean so much?"

"You wouldn't understand," he said.

"Try me."

"What's the use. The fact that you have to ask indicates that you don't see it at all." He sounded irritated with her and Dorothy let it drop. They were both silent for the next ten minutes or more. The moon, fuller, yellower than it had been the night before, softened the darkness, turned the sky into a pale backdrop; against it the swaying palm trees were black. Dorothy was thinking of Joanne and the inevitable icy reaction to the news that her father would be tied up Saturday and Sunday. She sighed. There had been a time when she was able to blame the failure of Gary's first marriage entirely on Vickie, but no longer. He was spoiled, petulant when crossed, demanding. . . . And she loved him. Damn, damn, damn, she thought, dreading the weekend.

Joanne Hazlett stared defiantly at her mother. "He'll talk to me this time, or I'll lose the sails out in the gulf, or get a hole in the gas tank, or something."

"Darling, I'm just warning you, don't count too much on it."

Joanne was so small, and slender, that she seemed younger than her seventeen years. Her waist-long hair made her look very much like Alice, Vickie was thinking, watching the barefoot girl pace furiously in the spacious apartment. Vickie was reminded of

Joanne at eighteen months, stamping her fat foot, ordering imperiously, "Do it!" She wondered what would happen when Gary and Jo actually got on a collision course. They would, sooner or later. They were too alike to avoid it much longer, each one demanding the universe make way for him, each one refusing to be deterred from whatever path he happened to be on at any particular time. Thank God, she thought, that Jo is as tough as Gary is. And more resilient.

"Honey," she said, "just one thing. Then I have to be going. If there is a snag. If Gary is tied up, or something comes up and you don't get to talk to him, you might consider talking to Dorothy. I'm sure that she would see your side."

"Oh, Mother, for heaven's sake! Are you serious? Ask her for help?" Joanne was brought up short. She stared at Vickie. From the kitchen the dishwasher, changing cycles to rinse, sounded like an airplane landing in the apartment.

Vickie glanced at her watch and stood up. "Honey, I really do have to go. I told Walter I'd be in the lobby at nine. I won't be late. We're going to catch the show, then have a bite to eat and come back home. We'll talk some more if you're still up." She drew on white doeskin gloves and glanced at herself in the hall mirror. Looking past her own image, she said to her daughter, "Don't keep blaming her, Jo. It shows a certain immaturity in you, you know. People get lonesome. I can't blame her. Or Gary. It just happens, that's all." She blew a kiss and left.

Joanne didn't move until she was alone in the apartment, listening to the noisy dishwasher, and, beyond the outer door, the creaky elevator. Then she threw herself down on the couch and pounded the end pillow with her fist. "Damn," she muttered. "God damn it all to hell." Her mother and Walter? Was that the message? Walter, that smooth-faced hypocrite? She knew they were meeting in the lobby at Walter's insistence, to avoid friction, keep things as smooth as possible between them. Would they spend the week-end together? She sat upright, shocked at the thought, accepting it. Her mother and Walter. Her father and Dorothy. Plastic, all of them. All of them pretending so hard, all of them so phony, always playing roles, being so nice and polite, and all the time just waiting for her to be out of the way so they could let down the masks, be themselves. She tried to imagine what her mother was like apart from her, alone with Walter, and she couldn't. Another person, a stranger to her. She had sneaked into the hallway of the beach house once when a party was going on, just before the separation, and she had seen her mother standing close to a man who had his arm around her shoulder. There were others in the group, and now she knew that it had been meaningless, but then, at twelve, she had been frightened and indignant. She had wanted to run to them, to wrench his hand from her mother. She had searched the crowds for her father, wanting to warn him, to tell him to protect her mother, and when she had found him, in the midst of another group, his head had been close enough to touch the silver hair of another woman. Mrs. Joyner.

Was that why her mother was willing for her to go to Europe alone after finishing school? Expecting a fight, she had found no resistance at all. "I'm going one way or another. I want to live in France, for a year at least, and study art. I want to travel to Germany and Spain, and Norway, and . . . everywhere. If you and Dad won't let me, then I'll run away and go."

"Honey, isn't that a little drastic? I think it's a good idea. I'm on your side."

Joanne had felt cheated. All her beautiful arguments unused, unasked for. Her mother had balked only at seeking permission from Gary for the trip. "That's up to you, darling. I can't afford to finance it, and I can't argue your cause with him any longer."

"But he'll say no. He thinks I'm a baby."

"Then it's up to you to convince him that you know what you want, and that this is it."

Joanne stared ahead dry-eyed and wondered if her mother had secretly been relieved to get rid of her for the next year or two, knowing that after that she probably would be working, or back in college, or married, or at any rate out of her hair. She turned to stare at the hall mirror and saw again her mother standing there. Hair so beautifully coiffed, dyed, of course; make-up hiding her skin, her body shaped by diet, exercise, and a one-piece girdle and bra, her hands hidden by white gloves, her legs sheathed in flesh-colored nylon. Even her eyes had been covered, by contact lenses. For a terrifying moment she wondered if there had been anything behind all the layers. Would it be like stripping away the bandages of the invisible man, revealing only air beneath? She touched her own face, and ran her other hand down her body, pressing in hard, as if checking her own substance.

She was afraid to go to sleep until she heard her mother return home; Walter was with her. Joanne lay in her bed and waited for the elevator noise to tell her that Walter was gone again. She dozed and later awakened, frightened, and sat upright, unable to say what had awakened her, what had frightened her. A dream, she told herself. She got up and went to her mother's door and opened it quietly. She could see the dark head, covered with soft curlers, a shiny cheek that was soaking up a nutrient cream. Her mother sighed in her sleep and Joanne closed the door again, not certain of what she had expected to see. Even asleep her mother had seemed unreal and hollow.

Joanne pinched her leg until it hurt when she got back in bed. "I am real," she said softly. "I know I am real." The fear persisted and she knew it was because she doubted. How could she be real, if her mother wasn't? Why should she be real? Nobody else was. Nobody at all.

Hank Pinelli sipped beer, his own home brew, and watched Gary Hazlett. Hank was five feet nine, twenty years older than Gary, fifty pounds lighter, but he always felt that he was watching a child when Gary Hazlett was with him. Gary was walking around the large table that held Hank's village. Looking down on it was like looking into swimming pools filled with nothing, surrounded by greenery, sidewalks, streets. Gary turned away and backed up several steps, then looked again. From this angle windows glowed yellow, street lights cast unwavering light in tiny circles, a train wound about the streets, paused in the small red station, gathered speed once more, then slowed to enter the town at the far end and retraced its route. Every building, the train, cars, all were topped by bits of black material that seemed more like holes cut from the scene than like coverings. Over the village a single two hundred watt bulb burned.

"You've done something new to it," Gary said, studying the scene.

"There's always something that can be done." Hank lifted the black roof from a square building and inside were seats and a stage. "Entertainment," he said, grinning. The underside of the roof was a maze of wires, and minuscule wafers that gleamed when he turned it. He replaced it and picked up his half quart stein once more.

"Look, Hank, you know what I'm after. You know that Cramer wants to work with you on the military aspects of this, with the holograms. Are you going to Davenport's party Tuesday night?"

Hank shrugged. "He asked me, and I said I'd let him know." Gary felt a twinge of jealousy at the easy-going relationship between the two old men. Davenport hadn't given him the option of attending or not. Hank drained his stein and put it down. "He doesn't want a government contract. You know that."

"God damn it, Hank. It could be the biggest thing

ever to come out of the company. No one would be hurt any by it."

"No one?"

"Look, Hank, I'm authorizing you and Cramer to work up a demonstration of the plastic coupled with the holograms for Tuesday night. Cramer says he can do it, if you cooperate."

"I don't believe you have the power to authorize such a demonstration, Mr. Hazlett."

Hank lifted his stein and looked surprised to find it empty. He crossed the lab to the far side where a large wooden keg was on the counter amidst flasks and stacks of plastic chips. He filled the stein again, drank and wiped the foam from his mouth before he looked at Gary. "Beer?"

"No." Gary followed him across the room. "I'm issuing a direct order, Hank. I am the director of research of this company, you know. I do have the authority."

Hank chuckled deep in his throat and drank again. "Me, I don't know nothing about holograms and such, Gary, but I do know that invisibility as a visual quality only don't mean a thing nowadays. So we absorb the radar and infrared, and everything else you throw at it, but don't you see, boy, that's the same as sending it back. The message is the same."

"You let me worry about that end of it," Gary said. "I know what I'm doing."

"I wonder. You know, Gary, lot of times things that seem one way have a way of turning, shifting ground so to speak, and suddenly it's a new picture altogether. Hard to know what's real and what only appears real until you lean out and try to touch it, handle it, work with it. Then you close a fist on air."

"Just say it, whatever it is you're driving at."

"Nothing, Gary. Nothing." He chuckled again and said, "I'll let you know. Got me a fishing date for this weekend, and that won't leave much time before Tuesday night."

Gary tried to relax his throat. He felt as if every muscle in his stomach and chest had been squeezed. It was that damn chuckle. That was the way Davenport treated him, like a small boy with golden curls, who was always wrong, but tolerated in spite of it. Pinelli with his toy village that he loved more than anything in the outside world; Davenport with his plans for the celebration coming up in another week or so, two old men dreaming away their lives, playing with illusions, laughing at the young men who were practical, who were looking ahead to a time when Davenport wouldn't control the company, to a time when the only men in the laboratories would be qualified scientists with the proper training and degrees. Pinelli went to the wall switches and turned off the two hundred watt bulb above his village. The batteries had enough energy stored to continue to light the tiny houses and buildings. He turned another switch to "off" and the village went out.

"Damn you, Pinelli, what are you doing? You never leave this lab. You live here seven days a week. You wouldn't know which end of a fishing rod to hold."

" 'Bout time I learned something practical like that, wouldn't you say?" Hank put down his beer and went to the hall door. "I'll be in touch with you, Gary. On Monday."

Gary stared at him another moment, then stamped from the lab, back to his office through deserted halls and past empty desks where typewriters were covered neatly and only the muted hush of the air-conditioner could be heard. Cramer was waiting for him.

"Get down there and talk to him before he has a chance to get out," Gary said. The other man shrugged and left. He was in his twenties, string-beanlike, with large glasses and long nervous hands. He had a Ph.D. in physics, and he was afraid of Hank Pinelli.

Sitting behind his desk, watching the door shut in slow, silent motion, Gary knew that he was afraid of Pinelli, and of Davenport, and that his was the fear of a child who knows he is pushing his parents too hard too fast, but is unable to stop. He did have the authority. No one else in the research department questioned it. He knew exactly what was going on in each of the labs. Who else could have pulled the separate projects together to come up with this new idea? No one, not even the old man. If he didn't have the authority to give Pinelli a direct order, what was he there for? Pinelli was only one of a dozen scientists working for the company. Six years now he'd had his own way, no one interfering, no one asking for justification for the expenses, and this one time that Gary did ask, direct, the old fool questioned his authority. Drumming his fingers on the desk, he knew that Pinelli would refuse to cooperate, and that, if he took the matter to Davenport, the old man would back his crony without a hearing, even if the matter happened to be one that the old man approved of. Okay, he'd go ahead, not wait until Pinelli turned him down. Let the old fool leave town, be out of reach over the weekend. He didn't yet have a private lock on his lab, and Gary had company keys. They'd go ahead without him. He must have stacks of the black roofing material ready to install. Let Cramer earn his salary by working overtime. He rubbed his eyes with the back of his hand, and saw again the little rectangles of nothingness, the moving strip of nothingness that was the top of the train. He imagined an entire city covered with the stuff, crisscrossed so that rain could enter through the interstices, but to the eye presenting mile after mile of the abyss. The picture became more real, and he felt himself dropping toward that abyss, falling down into the void where nothing was or ever had been or ever would be. He jumped up, kicking his chair back into the wall with a reassuring crash. He was shaking.

Perry Davenport was a relaxed seventy-one-year-old man. He walked around Tony Freemac appraisingly and touched his beard, testing the growth. "Coming along nicely, boy," he said. "Another week or ten days and you can start shaping it. The spitting image you'll be of him. Most remarkable likeness."

Tony also touched the stubby beard. "Mr. Davenport, any dark man with a beard is pretty much like any other dark man with a beard."

"That's what I thought until I started to search for the right man," the old man said. "Not true. You need the right bony structure, big bones, a broad face, wide forehead. I'm telling you, my boy, my grandfather was a real man. Big, broad, strong. A real man. And you're the spitting image of him."

Perry Davenport was a broad man, or had been, and was now in the process of shrinking slightly. His white hair was thick and coarse and much too long. Somewhere in his past he had acquired a navy blue skull cap, which he wore whenever he went outside, and he was proud of the fact that in twelve years now he'd worn shoes and socks only one time, at the funeral of an old friend. Nothing else could get him out of the sandals he favored. His knees were knobby, his white shorts dirty, and his chest was bare and brown, with a sprinkling of white hair. He didn't look much like a millionaire, or the president of an internationally known plastics company.

"Well, breakfast will be ready in five minutes, son. Had your dip yet?"

Tony nodded. "Yes, sir. An hour ago."

"Having trouble sleeping?"

"Not really. I've been getting up early, trying my hand with the morning light. It's different then." Tony glanced at the side of his room where he had canvases turned toward the wall. The old man's glance followed his. He didn't ask to see the paintings.

After a moment the old man said, "See you in the sunroom, five minutes." He left through the doors to the porch and strode down the beach into the surf. A minute later he was swimming vigorously, straight out. He dived, surfaced, turned, and swam back. Tony watched him a moment and, whistling, went to inspect his new beard in the bathroom mirror. He didn't care if the old man was nutty, he liked him, and the job was paying better than anything he'd ever done in the past.

Before he left his room he turned the canvas around and stared at it, perplexed by it, by himself. Never before had he attempted formless color and light, and he was ready to admit that he couldn't do it. It was like putting a punched card into a black box only to find that the holes weren't right, and not be able to see what was right. The times it did fit, the black box gave him a pleasurable feeling, and all he was getting from this painting was disquieting thoughts, uneasiness, an urge to rip it to pieces, to burn it, to take his easel out and try again. There had to be a communication line from the black box to his hands, a line that bypassed his consciousness usually, and he felt that the line had been disconnected. He backed away and squinted. There were broad streaks of green shading to black, flecked with gold, and another streak of gold, with something else coming through, as if the gold were nearly translucent. He wasn't satisfied with it, but he didn't know what was wrong, or what he had been trying to do, or how to fix it. He decided that in the morning he would start over. Unhappy, he swung the canvas to the wall once more and turned to leave his room. Glancing outside, he saw the old man wade from the rolling waves, and stop, looking up the beach. A tall, slender woman joined him and they stood at the edge of the water talking. The old man put his arm about her shoulders and seemed to aim her at the house, and they walked toward it together. The woman—a girl actually—must have been out swimming also, Tony decided, when they got closer. She was wearing a white, short tunic and sandals, and she swung a bathing cap by its strap.

When Tony arrived on the sunporch, she was seated

at the breakfast table. "Hi," he said, "Mr. Davenport dressing?"

"Yes. I'm Dorothy Hazlett." She looked sick and when she lifted her cup, her hand shook so hard the coffee almost spilled.

"Tony Freemac." He poured coffee and sat down with it. Mrs. MacIntyre appeared with a covered dish that she placed before him.

"You're sure now, Mrs. Hazlett? Toast maybe?" she asked.

"No thanks. I really did have breakfast already."

Tony felt her stare, and consciously kept his fingers away from the new beard. He lifted the cover from his dish and the old man came out to the porch, followed closely by the cook-housekeeper.

"Ah, sausage and apple rings," Davenport said.

Mrs. MacIntyre made a sound like a horse snorting and lifted the silver lid. There were two poached eggs on his plate. "I'll give you sausage," she said. "Like fun I will."

The old man winked at Dorothy. "I bewitched her into thinking I'm eating some bland tasteless concoction that she made," he said, "and all the while she is preparing exactly what I like most." He ate with gusto.

Again Tony felt Dorothy's gaze and he turned deliberately to look out at the ocean.

"Mr. Freemac, I'm sorry. I've been staring. You remind me so much of someone else." She stood up and held out her hand to Davenport. "I really have to go." She looked at the clock behind Davenport and shook her head slightly. There was a frown on her forehead and for a moment she looked as if she were going to faint. Tony watched her closely, but she seemed to gather herself together again.

"Honey, you just sit right back down there and wait for me to finish eating. Then I'm going to drive you back to your place."

"I'm due at the airport in half an hour." She said, "I . . . I'll call a taxi."

"Yeah, like fun you will," the old man said. "Just sit."

"I'll drive you home," Tony said. He wondered how she had got to the house.

As if sharing his wonder, she said, "It's about six or seven miles down the beach."

"You swam that far?" His tone said he didn't believe it.

"I couldn't have."

Davenport pushed his chair back then. He looked at Dorothy closely, then yelled, "Mrs. Mac, bring some more coffee for the young lady." To Dorothy he said, "You want to talk?"

"Mr. Davenport, I feel such a fool. I don't know how I got here. I guess I walked, but . . ." She shook her head and turned to Tony. "And you. . . . I thought at first that I had met you down on the beach two nights ago. Did I?"

He shook his head. She nodded, as if to herself. "I'll call a cab now and go back home. I don't want to interrupt you any more than I have already, Mr. Davenport."

Davenport stood up also and led the way from the room, talking as he went. "I'm going down that way, want to see Hank Pinelli. You just wait a minute while I get a shirt on, young lady. And don't you touch the telephone. I've been wanting to get to know you better. Ever thought of writing a biography? Y'know I've paid a mint on research. Hate to see it go to waste." At the door she turned and looked again at Tony, as if begging him to remember. He shook his head ruefully.

"Good-by," she said, and followed Davenport into the hallway.

Tony took his coffee to his room with him and again turned the canvas around to study it. He thought he knew what was wrong with it suddenly, and he put the cup down on a low table, and got out his brushes. When Mrs. MacIntyre knocked to tell him that lunch was ready he stepped back to look at what he had done. He had a violent headache, and his fingers were stiff, but he had got it. Something. There was a marble city, empty, cold, and beautiful, and one figure, a woman, whose posture said that she was lost and alone and afraid. Her face was in shadow, only her attitude spoke, and it was eloquent. He had captured the greens and blacks, and had the gold where it belonged, leading away, up and away from the emptiness of the street scene.

The woman he had painted was Dorothy Hazlett. He stared at it, and even with the face hidden, he knew that shape, the carriage, the way her hands were held. He started to paint her out of the scene, but he stopped and withdrew his hand. He felt very tired. When Mrs. MacIntyre knocked again, he was sprawled out on the bed sound asleep.

Small hideous men squatted about a carcass tearing at the bloody meat with their hands. Naked, hairy, only their eyes and the purposefulness of their arrested motions gave them humanity. Dorothy stared at the illustration in fascination. Gone without a trace, their history a surmise only, an artist's conception of what their lives must have been like, if they actually had existed at all.

A row of artifacts headed the page and she studied them: bits of rough-hewn rock, shaped by hands? Weather? Tumbling? Shaped by machines? She looked past the page to see machines turning out artifacts, sending them along conveyor belts through aging rays, to other belts that carried them over the surface of the earth and deposited them. There was a three-dimensional screen with an unfocused image being resolved on it. The image firmed, became sharp-edged and real. It was a flint ax. As she watched, the ax floated against a black backdrop, settled, and the background filled in forming a forest scene, the remains of a fire pit at the edge of a cliff. Other artifacts were there, half buried in the soil, partially covered by pebbles, broken, with the pieces carefully arranged so that a whole could be discerned. The ax was positioned, one edge of it protruding from the ground, moss resolved over it, the entire scene panned briefly, then shifted to the black backdrop.

"Flight 104 now arriving Gate 12."

Dorothy shook herself awake and dropped the magazine she had been reading. She looked at the wall clock. Joanne's flight was half an hour late. The announcement was repeated and she knew that that was what had roused her. She hurried to Gate 12 in time to see the plane making its final turn and gliding to a stop. The ladder was rolled out, and presently Joanne was coming through the gate, looking past Dorothy, pretending not to be looking. She seemed too young, small, too vulnerable to be traveling alone.

"Hello, Jo. Your father couldn't make it. Business. How are you?" She wanted to hug the girl, but Joanne's shoulders stiffened, her head raised a fraction of an inch, and her smile became glazed and set.

"Oh? That's too bad. I'll just go pick up my bag. Be right back." Joanne didn't look again at Dorothy, but hurried off to the baggage claim counter. She wondered briefly what was wrong with her stepmother, who seemed pale and nervous, but didn't dwell long on it. In the car on the way to the beach house neither of them spoke much, and Joanne pretended to believe that Dorothy needed to concentrate on her driving. Once or twice she glanced at Dorothy's profile, and she wondered if she would be able ever to talk to her. Her stepmother was only ten years older than she was, very pretty, and really very nice. She couldn't help it if she hated her. Jealous of her, she corrected bitterly. Shows a certain immaturity, don't you know. She wondered if Dorothy was sick, or pregnant. She savored the full bitterness of having her stepmother pregnant, and she caught herself hoping it was true, visualizing her stepmother dying in childbirth.

Nothing changes, Joanne thought. Edwards' store, the out-of-phase red light that had always seemed stuck on red, the smells, gulls above wheeling. . . . Dorothy said hesitantly, "Jo, if your father can't find the time to take the boat out with you . . ." And even that was right out of the past, same words, different speaker.

"Oh, I didn't really want to go sailing," Joanne said quickly. "That was just an excuse to come visit." It sounded like she was afraid that Dorothy was going to offer to go out with her, she realized too late. She glanced up in time to see Dorothy looking at her, and for a moment their gazes met and held. Dorothy smiled faintly and nodded.

"Okay," she said, and Joanne wanted to cry.

Joanne snorkeled lazily over the sand bar that paralleled the coast line for miles up and down the gulf. She made a right turn to get out of the path of a small inboard motorboat, but it turned also, and she lifted her head from the water and motioned to it to go away. A man yelled, "Are you crazy? What are you doing out here alone?"

He drew closer to her, and half crouching, made ready to throw a life preserver.

"What the bloody hell is the matter with you?" she shouted back at him. "Get that boat out of the way."

He stopped his movements with the white doughnut and stared at her. She replaced the snorkel and turned face down once more. She watched the shadow of the boat. He had turned off the motor and was keeping even with her, using a small paddle. Again she surfaced. "Why don't you go drown yourself somewhere else?"

"I thought you were a kid in trouble out here," he shouted back. "I came to rescue you."

She couldn't stop the sudden laughter that shook her. She pushed the face mask up on her head and said, "Right, and now you know that I'm not a kid in trouble. So you are dismissed. Okay?"

"So why not let me rescue you? I'm primed for a rescue job."

She glanced at him, young, bearded, very dark. She kicked herself toward the boat. "Okay. Rescue me already."

Sitting on the sea wall of the Davenport house he said, "But I did meet her this morning. Short, wavy, dark hair. Dark blue eyes. Twenties, tall, stacked. Right?"

"And I'm saying that's impossible. You lost a day somewhere. She met my plane this morning. She was at the airport before ten. And we didn't get back here to the beach until almost twelve."

She was drinking a lemonade, and he had a can of beer. Joanne finished her drink quickly and put the glass down. "I have to be going. No one knows where I am."

"Can I see you later?"

"Why?

"Why do you think? I think you're a crazy kid. I want to show you my paintings."

"No etchings?"

"Don't be funny."

She shrugged, thinking of her father's reaction to her dating a bearded man and nodded. "Sure. Why not? After dinner. Do you have a car or should I borrow one and come up here?"

"I'll pick you up. Nine o'clock?"

They swam to the small motorboat and he took her back down the beach. Clouds had filled the sky to the west, and the setting sun lighted them from behind, making them seem alive, writhing with color, outlined with bold strokes of silver and gold. He cut the motor close to the shore so that when she slid from the boat she was in waist-deep water. She waved to him and waded in carrying her mask, flippers, and snorkel.

Dorothy was pacing up and down the walk that edged the garden when Joanne came into view. Dorothy bit her lip, then said, "I was starting to worry about you."

Joanne stopped and looked up at her stepmother. "I'm sorry," she said suddenly. "I should have called you, but I didn't think of it. I met a house guest of Mr. Davenport's and we were talking."

Dorothy smiled faintly. "We've been calling him the reincarnation of Mr. Davenport's grandfather," she said. "No one has met him yet. He's the surprise guest for a dinner Tuesday night."

"But . . ." Joanne stopped the sentence. Why had Tony Freemac lied about meeting her stepmother that morning? Such a blatant lie, so easily swept aside. Or, was Dorothy lying now about him? Had they met? Not this morning, of course, but another time? She shrugged and fell into step beside Dorothy. "Is Dad going to be home for dinner?"

"Yes, but he's bringing someone with him. He's tied in knots about getting a contract from the government, and it seems that Mr. Davenport is so involved in this celebration of his that he just doesn't care about the real business of the company right now. Your father is in a tizzy over it all."

"Wouldn't you know that I'd choose such a rotten time to come to him with my problems." Joanne kicked sand hard and scowled.

Dorothy looked at her quickly, wondering if she had been invited to substitute for Gary. She wished that she were a few years older, more motherly, or that she and Joanne had got off to a better start back in the beginning. No one else on earth could make her feel so out of place and unwanted and awkward.

"Joanne," she started, "I . . . if you want to talk about something. I mean if I can arrange it so that Gary realizes that you have to talk to him, I'll try."

"Thanks," the girl said. "I have to talk to him. To both of you, I guess. Maybe tomorrow before I have to get my flight back."

Gary and Donald Cramer were sitting in the living room with martinis when Dorothy and Joanne joined them. Cramer was leaning forward talking intently, his thin face set in lines of concentration. He stood up belatedly, as if manners had been hard to learn and then not very well. Joanne kissed her father, nodded to the young man, and made polite noises when the introductions were made. Cramer wished they hadn't come into it. He didn't know how to talk with women, even when they were as young as Joanne, or as firmly married as Dorothy. He finished his martini and waited for the rest of them to carry the conversation.

"Donald is the new physicist I was telling you about, honey," Gary said, moving to the bar. Dorothy shook her head when he indicated the pitcher. "He'll be working with Hank Pinelli on that new process I was telling you about."

"The plastic abyss," Dorothy murmured. "Will a demonstration be ready for Tuesday night?"

Cramer looked startled and reached hurriedly for the new drink that Gary had poured. "I think so," he said.

Joanne sat quietly and Dorothy turned to her and said, with a touch of irony, "Dr. Cramer is creating illusions in the lab. Somehow it seems strange, doesn't it, to train a man, put him through graduate school, spend thousands of dollars on his education so that he can manipulate lights in such a way as to confuse the senses, tell you you're seeing what isn't really there. The old Indian rope trick done with holograms."

Gary laughed, and again there was an edge to his voice. Joanne felt her interest sharpen and she looked from her father to her stepmother. Before he could reply to her, the cook announced dinner and they all went to the dining room.

Tony Freemac arrived before they had finished dinner and Joanne made the introductions gleefully, watching his face when she said, "And my stepmother, Dorothy." Dorothy nodded easily, smiled, and indicated a chair.

"Won't you have coffee, Mr. Freemac?"

He looked from her to Joanne, bewilderment crossing his face. "Mrs. Hazlett, haven't we met?"

Dorothy studied him closely, then shook her head. "I don't know. On the beach?"

He shrugged and looked quickly toward Gary, and then turned his attention to his coffee, as if he thought Dorothy was hiding something from her husband. He looked embarrassed. Joanne let her gaze take in Dr. Cramer, and she wondered at the difference between the two men, both the same age, different in every other way. Tony, she knew from their brief talk, was a perpetual drop-out, and probably an artist. Cramer had decided on his goal very early and had not deviated from it once. She was paying little attention to the words being said, but watching the faces of those about her, and it seemed that she was withdrawing from them, becoming more remote, less a participant than an observer. They were talking about the inevitable changes that had already been started and that would have to be finished before a desirable future could be planned and carried out.

"Like the population thing," Gary was saying. "It's too late now to control it. It's like a disease that has been allowed to get a hold on the patient. All anyone can do is wait for it to run its course, and then talk about preventive medicine. You don't start an immunization program when the patient is weak from illness. Possibly gasping his last breaths."

"All the problems that we point to and scream about are in the same category," Cramer said. "Pollution of the air and streams. Slums. Poverty. Inertia will carry them on to the logical conclusions. After they've gone to the extreme, then we can start over, from different premises."

"So we simply sit back on our asses and wait for millions of people to get sick and die?" Tony said.

"Of course not," Cramer said with a touch of impatience. "You don't let the patient suffer any more than is necessary. You administer palliatives, bathe him, relieve his fever if you can. But you admit that he is ill and you admit that you can't cure him at this point."

"And if the patient dies?" Dorothy asked.

"Then you have learned something new that can be used the next time," Gary said, ending the conversation. He finished his coffee and looked pointedly at Dr. Cramer.

To Joanne, who was watching them from a great distance now, it seemed that they were on stage, talking idly about nothing, playing their roles with finesse. She looked past them and examined the stage props: pale furnishings, heavy gold drapes, pale blue rugs. The stage hadn't been changed since she had left, was exactly as she remembered from her earliest days. She squinted and stared at the props, past them, and saw blackness.

". . . just get bigger and bigger, less suited to the people they are supposed to serve. Why do we let it happen?"

"The cities reflect what we teach our architects to admire. This is the age of technocracy. The cities reflect that." Gary's voice sounded faint and distant. Joanne didn't look at him, or at Dorothy, who answered.

"And the walls will rise higher and be polished and smooth and unbroken. Dark green, almost black. A person walking along such sidewalks, with such walls on all sides of him, will be lost. . . ."

Joanne forced her gaze to penetrate the blackness

that she saw, and the blackness was deep and endless, but forming in it now was a pale luminescence. She stared at it, and a shifting light seemed to steady itself, to take shape, as if images were coming into focus.

". . . lost from what? I don't know what you mean when you say something like that."

"Lost from humanity, maybe."

The light was not moving at all; it was as if gauze curtains were being dissolved, another stage, another set. A city.

"Man's humanity doesn't depend on his environment," Gary.

"But his humanity can be destroyed by it," Tony Freemac.

A city grew before her eyes, a city with tall green buildings that were cold and threatening. No one walked in the city.

"This whole thing could go on for hours and we would be where we were in the beginning. When we get down to finding out exactly what we all mean by humanity, what we mean by man even, then we might have a profitable discussion about what's happening to mankind." Gary stood up and put his napkin down precisely on the table.

"All our problems will fade away if we just solve the semantics first," Dorothy said softly, with a trace of sarcasm.

"Don, let's get to our work," Gary said impatiently. "You coming in, honey?"

Dorothy nodded. "In a few minutes."

Tony had leaned forward when Gary stood up, and he said, "You admit, Mr. Hazlett, that something is happening to mankind? Can you go that far?"

Gary laughed easily. The impatience was well hidden when he said, "Man has more time for introspection than he's ever had in the past. More navel searching results in more lint finding, more unraveling to attempt. Mankind is better off today than at any time since the beginning of life. Maybe some of us are too well off. Leaves too much time to brood."

He motioned to Cramer and they went to the study and closed the door behind them. Dorothy looked from Tony to Joanne, who was still withdrawn and abstracted. "Are you two going out?" she asked.

"Nothing special," Tony said. Joanne seemed to shake herself and turned her gaze from infinity to look at Dorothy. "That city you described, Mrs. Hazlett," Tony said after a moment, "have you seen it somewhere? A magazine or something?"

Joanne and Tony were both watching her. Dorothy shook her head. "I don't think so."

"I saw it," Joanne said suddenly.

"Where?" Tony turned to her.

Joanne stared once more at the gold drapes. She walked over to touch the heavy fabric, then she pulled the edge of it aside and touched the wall behind it. When she turned again, she seemed paler, less certain of herself. "I don't know," she said. "It was like a dream, with my eyes open. And wide awake."

Tony pushed his chair back then and stood up abruptly. "Mrs. Hazlett, will you come with us. I wanted to show Joanne some of my paintings. I'd like to show you one, too. It's of your city."

"Can't it wait until Tuesday night?" Dorothy asked, glancing at Joanne.

Joanne said quickly, "It's all right, Dorothy. There's something funny happening. And I don't mean funny-ha-ha. It's sort of scary."

Dorothy still hesitated. After a pause she said, "I'll come in my car. You two go on, I'll follow you."

All the exits had been made on cue: exit, stage left; exit, stage right; leaving Dorothy alone in the spotlight pondering the silverware. She didn't want to go look at Tony's painting. She didn't want to probe the strange things that were happening, the strange things she was thinking and feeling. It all seemed to tie in with the practical joke that Gary had played on her, mussing her bed, pretending she had been asleep when she had actually been on the beach walking with a man she was now certain had been Tony Freemac. Why didn't he admit that he had been there? And this morning. . . She shook her head. She especially didn't want to think about the morning. She had gone to meet Joanne. Period. And yet, her bathing suit was wet, her white sharkskin tunic was stiff with salt water, and she had a memory of something that hadn't happened. Or almost a memory—rather it was like a dimly remembered shadow, as substanceless as a shadow, but more persistent. She had met Joanne's plane. Exit Dorothy, stage right.

She and Joanne and Tony stared at the painting soundlessly. Dorothy realized that she had bitten blood from her lip only when she touched it and saw the red smear on her fingers. Joanne sat unmoving, her face white, her hands clenched hard in her lap.

"Telepathy," Joanne said through tight lips. "We've just had a practical demonstration of telepathy, and we're all scared to death by it."

"Somehow the three of us experienced this vision," Tony said. "You two saw it, I simply felt it. But telepathy is too simple."

"Simple?" Joanne sounded near hysteria. She couldn't take her eyes from the painting.

"Yes, simple. That doesn't explain how Dorothy could have been here this morning when she was also meeting you at the airport."

Dorothy started at his words. The memory that wasn't a memory, but a vision recalled. "What do you mean?"

"You were here," he said, and described her tunic, her bathing suit. "You were nervous, afraid. Mr. Davenport took you home." He rubbed his hand over the beard and wished for the first time that he had turned the old man down when he had approached him with the ridiculous proposal. The beard seemed obtrusive somehow, as if the old man had claimed him, given him colors, or a stamp of ownership.

Dorothy slowly shook her head. "You have to be wrong," she said. She had risen and was backing away from him, from the painting, groping behind her for the door. "That's crazy! First Gary, now you. . . . Why are you doing this?" She heard the rising tone of her voice and could do nothing to control it. Across the room, as if across a chasm, through clouds, she could see the chalky face of her stepdaughter. For an instant she reeled, and she heard Gary's voice: ". . . by eleven at the latest. Dinner will be over and his fool ceremony will be out of the way. In front of so many people, I don't think he'll put up too much of an objection, if you have everything ready to go. Okay?"

"I can have my end of it ready, but what about Pinelli? Won't he make a stink if we use his lab, his . . . ? Mrs. Hazlett, are you all right?"

"Yes, of course." She stared at the table in confusion. She had knocked over her wineglass, and sherry was spreading across the glossy surface of the table. She stood up abruptly. "How clumsy of me." Gary was mopping it up with his napkin, paying little attention to her, continuing his conversation with Dr. Cramer.

"I told you I'd see to Pinelli. Now look, there will be a stage, and that's perfect for the demonstration. . . ."

Dorothy watched his hands moving competently, cleaning up the spilled wine, and she tried to move her own fingers and found them chilled and stiff, as if she had allowed both hands to lie in an uncomfortable position so long that they had gone to sleep. Her mouth felt stiff, and there was a cold feeling about her face, her forehead. She sat down quickly.

"Dorothy!" Someone caught her arm and she was being led to a chair. Her head was being forced down. Voices nearby, but distant, indistinguishable, incoherent. After a moment she struggled to get up again.

"Sip some of this," Tony said. It was straight bourbon. She tasted it, then pushed the glass away.

"I want to call my house," she said.

"Wait a minute or two," Tony said. "Then I'll take you home if you want."

She shook her head and looked around for the telephone. "I have to call now. Right now." Again the rising note was there. She bit her lip and took a deep breath. "I'm all right, but I have to call this minute."

Tony looked helplessly at Joanne, but she was staring wide-eyed at Dorothy. She was pale down to her lips. "Okay," he said. "Joanne, will you get the number." He helped Dorothy up, and made certain that she was steady, and they went into the study where Joanne dialed. Dorothy took the phone from her before she finished the last number. Tony pulled the phone from Dorothy's ear so that they could all hear the rings. Joanne moved in closer. The ringing stopped, and from the other end of the wire, they could hear Dorothy's low-pitched voice: "Hello."

Gary looked up at Dorothy, standing at the telephone stand with a puzzled look on her face. "Who was it at this hour?" he asked. "Jo?"

"No. I don't know. They hung up."

"Wrong number. Bad enough during the day, but at eleven . . ." Gary laughed and turned back to Cramer and the sketch of Davenport's study. "Now, the stage is just about here. I haven't seen it since the construction started, but I saw the plans. It's small, about ten by ten, a foot higher than the room. That's the area that I want you to consider. How much equipment will it take? How long to set up your gear, and so on? How many men to get everything in place? Can you arrange that end of it? You understand?"

"Sure. I can handle that. Be a good idea if I could get in ahead of time. Get it all fixed up and just press the light switch to start the show. More impressive that way."

Dorothy thought: reality needs more than a button to start it, Doctor.

Gary said, "On the stage there's going to be a judge's desk, a chair, and off to the side a gallows. Period. Look at the sketch again. The stage backs onto the porch, with a double door there. While you are projecting your images, we will open that door, and rearrange the stage."

Peel away curtains and find other sets, other stages, other curtains. How many layers? Dorothy heard the car stop on the pebble drive and stood up. The cook had gone home hours ago. Neither Gary nor Cramer had heard anything. Gary's pale hair and the doctor's thin face side by side like a Dali distortion, facets of the same thing, and the thing not what she had always called man before. She rose and walked from the room without drawing the attention of either of them. In the hallway she paused, and instead of going to the entrance, she turned and went into the bedroom and undressed quickly, and got into bed.

Tony and Joanne argued briefly. "Don't warn them with the doorbell," Joanne said. "Let me open it."

Dorothy stood to one side and waited silently. Tony looked at her worriedly and moved aside so that Joanne could fit her key into the lock. When the door swung open, Dorothy walked ahead of them to the study door. She opened it, turned, and smiled at them.

"You two are back early."

Tony felt the trembling in Joanne's arm and his fingers bit down hard. She moaned. "Yes, Jo forgot her purse." He studied Dorothy, but she seemed perfectly normal, smiling, almost amused by them, as if their paleness and jerky motions were signs of guilt at being caught reaching for forbidden cookies.

"Oh? Maybe it's in the living room." She moved ahead of them and glanced about. "Did you call a few minutes ago?"

Joanne shook her head, staring at Dorothy, her

pallor so obvious now that Dorothy looked from her to Tony and then back. Very gently she asked, "Are you all right, Jo? Is anything wrong?" She took a step toward the girl, Joanne backed away.

"I'm fine. Fine. It must be in the car," she said quickly and wheeled about and ran from the room.

Dorothy started to follow, but Tony caught her arm. "Have you been here all night?"

"Of course. In the study with Gary and Dr. Cramer. Why?"

"I have to see Mr. Hazlett," he said. "It's important."

Dorothy closed her eyes for a second. "What is it?" she asked. "What's wrong?"

"I don't know. I have to see your husband, Dorothy." She looked surprised and alarmed at his tone, and the roughness of his grasp on her arm.

"I'll call him," she said. She left him in the living room and stood at the closed door for several seconds with her eyes shut. Why did he seem so familiar? Like someone she had known a long time ago, known well enough to trust. And why had Joanne acted as if she were terrified of her? She thought of the other night when they'd had guests, and slowly, with reluctance, she went down the hall to the bedroom she shared with Gary, and opened the door. She took only one step inside, enough to see that the bed was mussed, her pillow indented, her cigarettes on the table. . . .

Gary looked annoyed when she told him that Tony Freemac wanted to talk to him, but he got up and followed her to the living room. Joanne wasn't there. Dorothy didn't go in with Gary, but went to Jo's room and looked inside. She must have gone back to the car, looking for the purse. Dorothy saw Joanne opening her purse, taking a tissue from it, closing it again. They were in Davenport's study, and on the table the telephone, with Tony's hand covering it. Joanne pale, the echo of her scream still in the air. . . .

". . . out of here and stay out!"

"Ask Davenport. Ask Joanne. I'm telling . . ."

"You're telling me nothing. I'll call the police if you don't get out of here!"

She ran down the hall to the living room. Tony and Gary were standing face to face yelling at each other. Dr. Cramer emerged from the study, and Joanne materialized from the back of the hall. "What's going on?" Cramer asked.

"Nothing. Freemac is leaving," Gary said.

"Dad, you have to believe him!" Joanne cried. "I saw her. I was with her, and then she . . . she pretended . . ."

"Joanne, get to your room. And you, get out!"

"You won't listen because you're afraid to," Joanne screamed. "Who is posing as Dorothy? Why is she pretending that she doesn't even know Tony? Who met me this morning?"

Dorothy caught the doorjamb and steadied herself. They were all so distant, their faces distorted by rage and fear, mouths opening and closing with nothing coming out. And behind them yawned the blackness, but none of them seemed to see it, to be aware that it was there. Her fingers clutching the doorjamb began to slip through it, and the wood melted away until her fingers met, and there was nothing to hold her up. She slid to the floor.

"Dorothy!" Gary lifted her from the floor and turned furiously to Tony. "See what you've done with your crazy talk. Now will you get out of here." He carried her to the bedroom and put her down and sat at her side gently rubbing her wrist.

"I'm all right," she said. "I didn't faint."

"Hush, darling. Just relax and rest."

She closed her eyes and felt hot tears gathering behind the lids. "Gary, what's happening? Am I going insane?"

His hand holding hers clenched, hurting her fingers. "Don't say that. It's that crazy kid out there. That bum that Davenport picked up."

The tears were being squeezed out. "I didn't faint," she said again. "There wasn't anything to stand on. Nothing to lean against. I fell down."

"Honey, stop. Just stay perfectly still. I'm going to go get you a sleeping pill. Now, don't move until I get back."

The tears were hot on her face, cold on her neck. She tried to stop them and couldn't. She was making no sound, but the tears wouldn't stop flowing.

She swallowed the capsule he brought her, and she lay with his hand stroking her forehead, her cheek. Thinking: Some of us need so many others to finish us. He needs others, like a colonial organization, or is it organism. One segment, all can survive but it isn't finished, isn't whole, and it knows, knows, and tries to find others it can fuse with, even if only temporarily. I almost complete him, sometimes I am enough for a while, it doesn't last. But I am complete. Drifting alone in the sea. Whole, sometimes splitting, becoming two, one to go this way, one that, each complete. Drifting on the surface only, never penetrating, sometimes seeing a break, seeing the bottomless sea that we are afloat on, seeing the layers and layers that we could peel away if we knew how. Surface tension keeping us in place, but others can pierce it, dive beneath it, rise above it. It's not a boundary to them. We're like water beetles skating along, never aware that the real world lies beneath. . . .

Gary stroked her forehead and watched her face. The tears stopped and gradually she relaxed, and took a long sighing breath. Her hand clutching his relaxed its grip, and fell away, the fingers curled. Very gently he wiped her cheeks and smoothed back her hair wet with tears. His hands were tender as he undressed her, and then pulled the sheet over her.

Tony, Joanne, and Donald Cramer were in the living room, not talking, but anxious, and apparently they had been talking. Cramer looked upset, and Joanne and Tony were sitting together defensively on the couch.

"Is she all right?" Joanne asked.

"I gave her a pill. She's asleep now."

"I guess I should be going." Cramer stood up.

"Wait a minute," Gary said. "Have you talked to him?" He indicated Tony. Cramer hesitated a moment and then nodded. "What do you make of it?"

"Nonsense, of course." Cramer glanced toward Joanne and smiled nervously. "Not deliberate, I think, but still . . ."

"You're a fool," Joanne said icily. "Why would we make up such a story? Wait until Mr. Davenport backs it up, and he will. He was with her this morning. He'll tell you."

"Honey, don't rely on the old man," Gary said. "He could be taken in too." He went to the bar and poured Scotch into four glasses, added soda, and handed one to Tony and one to his daughter. He got the other two and gave one of them to Cramer. Joanne held hers without testing it. "You need it," he said, and took a deep drink of his own. "Freemac, I'm sorry I blew up at you. We have to get to the bottom of what's going on, and that isn't the way. Now, you two say that Dorothy was with you in Davenport's house this evening. I say that she was here all night. Someone is mistaken, or . . ." He stopped and swirled his drink for several seconds before adding, "Or, someone is playing a monstrous hoax that is potentially very dangerous to Dorothy. And that brings up the question of why anyone would impersonate her for your benefit. I know that I couldn't be fooled by an impersonator, but you don't know her that well, Jo. You've been with her very little. And Freemac is a stranger to her. But why?"

"Daddy, I saw her go to the door of the study, turn around and pretend that she had been in there all night. She did it herself."

"How, honey? I knew she was here." He stopped

suddenly and stared past his daughter. A few nights ago. She'd sworn she was out when he knew she was home.

Tony said, "She asked me if she had met me on the beach one night recently. She seemed to think she had, but I wasn't out there. Was there another time that this happened, Mr. Hazlett? A couple of nights ago?"

"I don't know," Gary said.

Cramer swallowed the rest of his drink and put the glass down. "If it's not a mistake, it's a hoax," he said. "I don't know how or why, but she wasn't in two places at the same time. There has to be someone else involved in it for reasons that we don't know yet."

"Axiomatic, isn't it, Doctor, that no one person can be in two places at the same time. Just like it's axiomatic that two parallel lines can't meet? That the shortest distance between two points is a straight line? That the sun and moon go around the earth? Has this particular axiom ever been proven? Or even questioned?"

"Good God," Cramer said in disgust. "Some things don't need more proof than is supplied by a sane mind."

Tony laughed darkly. "I know what I saw," he said. "And if something has to go, it's the goddam law of physics, not the evidence of my eyes."

"The least reliable evidence there is."

"Maybe." Tony leaned forward and added, "But I saw Dorothy Hazlett drop one role and pick up another. I saw and talked with her this morning at the same time Jo saw and talked with her thirty miles away."

Gary rubbed his hand across his eyes and stood up. "Let's leave it for tonight. Jo, you look exhausted. Go on to bed, honey. I'll see you tomorrow, Don. And Freemac, tomorrow afternoon, about four? Can you come over for a drink then?"

He sat up drinking Scotch and soda, wandering to

the bedroom to stare at Dorothy now and again. She slept without movement. The sleeping pill was a strong one, too strong for her probably. She'd wake up feeling drugged and dopey. Finally he undressed and turned off the bedroom lights, and there was only moonlight in the room. Once more he stopped at the side of her bed; this time he dropped to his knees and buried his head in the sheet next to her warm body. "Please, please," he said. "Dorothy, I need you so much. Please, don't leave me. Please."

The sun was high and hot. Jo's shoulders were beginning to feel prickly, and she sat up and reached for a towel. Dorothy was just stepping onto the sand. "Here she comes," Joanne said. Tony sat up then. Joanne looked frightened.

"It's nearly noon," Dorothy said. "Your father really socked it to me with a mickey last night, didn't he?"

She went past them into the water, waded out until it was above her waist and then swam with a strong regular stroke. "She's rather terrific," Tony said, watching the white cap bobbing on the water.

"Yes. You'd think nothing ever happened to look at her now. She's always like that. Nothing ever throws her for long."

"Did she do something to you, or is this the stepdaughter syndrome showing?"

Joanne laughed. "Stepdaughter syndrome," she said. "I'll have to remember that. What a handy catch-all." He turned to look at her. "She's been very decent actually. More than I deserved, I guess."

"Okay. Just wondered."

"It's hard not to keep playing the game I made up."

"It must be."

"Let's swim."

Dorothy was dog paddling around the breakwater when they joined her. She looked surprised, then pleased to see them, and she pointed at a small hole in the concrete wall. A ten-inch octopus tentacle writhed. Joanne laughed and touched it, and it withdrew into the hole. They trod water waiting for it to reappear, but it didn't and finally they headed back to shore.

Dorothy toweled herself and lighted a cigarette. She didn't sit down. "I'm starving," she said, heading toward the house; she swung back around. "I don't know exactly what happened, not as much as anyone else it seems, but whatever it is, I'm not playing a joke. I'm not doing it."

"I don't think anyone is suggesting that, Dorothy," Tony said. He looked as if he hadn't slept at all. Dorothy saw that Joanne was equally exhausted. Probably she was the only one who had slept.

Joanne said, "How is Dad this morning? Does he think you're playing a trick on him?"

Dorothy shrugged. "He seems to think that I can stop all this nonsense if I want to." She laughed suddenly and tossed her cigarette away. "I suppose you could say he wants me to pull myself together." Joanne looked startled, but Tony laughed. "Have you two had breakfast, lunch, brunch? Come on, let's eat."

"How can you laugh at it?" Joanne asked. "It's the most terrifying thing I ever heard of, and you laugh."

Dorothy stopped again. A haunted look had come over her face, leaving it pinched and very afraid. Quietly she said, "If I don't laugh at it, I'll go mad. You see, I don't know where I was last night. And I don't know who was sleeping in my bed when I went in to look at it. Someone had been." She was almost running as she led the way to the house.

"I stayed up talking to the old man last night," Tony said, spreading jam over toast. "He's delighted with this business. Can't wait to talk to you, and Gary, anyone else who might be able to add to the details. You'd think he had arranged it all, and was just finding out that it was paying off."

Dorothy wasn't eating much. She dabbled with her omelet, broke her toast into bits, and drank coffee. "Did he have any suggestions to make?"

"I don't know. He went on at some length about selective evidence to verify our view of reality. He asked if you write poetry. Do you?"

She shook her head. "Not since my first love light was blown out when I was twelve. I wrote an ode to lost love and the hopelessness of life."

"He says that it doesn't matter because you're living poetry." Joanne looked blank, and he shrugged. "I don't know what he meant, I'm just reporting. He's going to call you as soon as I pass the word that you're up and about."

Dorothy pushed her plate back and stood up. "I don't want to go into any of this with anyone." She walked to the screen door and stared over the ocean. "I keep wondering, what if I see her, the other one? Is it a doppelgänger? We hear about such things, read of them, shrug and go on. I mean what else can you do? We can't understand them or believe in them, or cope with them. You know, like poltergeists. We read of this or that family being torn up by poltergeist tricks. The stories die down, and we put it aside. It doesn't fit anywhere and we forget about it. I turned down an assignment once to do a series of articles about clairvoyance, telepathy, fortunetelling, the whole range, simply because I couldn't believe in any of it. I knew it would be such a debunking series that the editor would hand it back to me. He wanted a sympathetic treatment. Everybody wants to believe. But how? Seeing things at a distance or in the future. Who can believe in such things? How? Who can believe in a doppelgänger?"

From the open door to the hall another voice said, "And why don't those stories all die then? Doesn't matter how often they get buried, someone always digs 'em up again."

They turned to see Perry Davenport. "Dorothy, I'm

buttin' in where I ain't been invited. Might as well let me stay, seeing that I'm one of the interested parties." He glared at Tony. "And you, what's the matter, you couldn't find a dime to make one lousy phone call?"

Tony grinned and stood up. He started to introduce Davenport to Joanne, but the old man stopped him. He grabbed the girl and hugged her. "You always make me think of a truth that we generally forget," he said to the embarrassed girl. "The smallest berries most often are the sweetest." He kissed her soundly and put her back down on her chair. He pulled one out for himself and sat down and regarded Dorothy. "First of all, that wasn't no poltergeist, and it wasn't no doppelgänger. It was you that I talked to yesterday, brought back to this house and watched walk inside it. You're not going to get nowhere long's you keep talking 'bout what it wasn't. Now you tell me what you remember doing yesterday morning."

Dorothy shrugged helplessly and moved away from the screen. Walking back and forth on the terrazzo floor, hearing the soft click of heel taps and nothing else, she said after a moment, "I went to the airport and waited for Joanne's plane, and we came home."

"Not enough," the old man said. "More details."

"Why? What difference does it make? I was there! I was here! Or someone was. I have to take your word, yours and his, that you were with someone who seemed to be Dorothy Hazlett. I don't know who that was. I just know where I was."

The old man nodded. He helped himself to coffee. "Take it easy, honey. Just start with getting up and try to recall as much as you can about the morning, the drive, waiting for the plane. Okay? Are you sure that it's as real in your mind as you think it is?"

"Oh," Dorothy cried, and sat down across the table from him. Vehemently she said, "It was as real as this is right now. Why won't anyone understand that?" She closed her eyes and leaned back, suddenly tired.

Perry Davenport patted her hand. "Honey, I believe

it, but I don't think you do. Look at me, Dorothy."
She opened her eyes and met his gaze. "Honey, I've
seen a lot of phonies and a few real people in my
time. You're one of the few, Dorothy. I think you're
in trouble, and maybe I can help. Maybe not. I'd
like to try, if you'll let me. Will you?"

She nodded. "I'll try to fill it all in, but there's so
little. . . . I had breakfast out here. Orange juice,
coffee, an egg." She stopped and he smiled encourag-
ingly at her. "All right. I knew that I had to leave by
nine, and I have a fear of being late for something like
that, so I planned to be on my way by fifteen 'til
nine." She talked on and in speaking of the details,
they came back clearer and clearer: dreading the
weekend, hoping Jo wouldn't be upset because Gary
wouldn't be able to spend any time with her, and so
on. The drive, the announcement of the late arrival,
waiting, reading.

"What was the magazine?"

She frowned, trying to remember. "*Look*, or *Life*.
I'm not certain. There was a big story on paleontology.
I read that while I waited." She stopped, seeing again
the men-things squatting about a fire, seeing the machine turning out projections of artifacts. She smiled
and said, "I had a fantasy about faking history and
then the plan. . . ."

"Whoa, girl. Just stop a minute there." Davenport
leaned back, tilting his chair, and looked pleased. "This
little fantasy, what about it?"

Dorothy tried to recall as much as she could about
the fantasy. "Of course," she said when she felt that
she had wrung it dry, "it all goes back to Gary's pre-
occupation with this innovation he's thought up, and
the contract he's trying to get for the company."

"Starts there," Davenport said, "but you took it a
giant step farther."

She looked puzzled and he said, "Don't you see?
What Gary and Cramer are after is a three-dimensional
image to confuse the eyes as long as the energy is on

and the projectors work, and what you invented in the terminal is a four-dimensional image that would endure regardless of the energy and the projectors."

"Four dimensional? How?"

"Yours would endure in time, and that makes it about as substantial as anything you can see around you right now." He pounded the table. "Is it there, or does my brain furnish the details working with pure energy only? I don't know." He stood up suddenly. "The other times that you were reported in two places at once, can you recall the same kind of details about them?"

She nodded. "Of course."

"Were there fantasies involved in those instances?"

"I don't remember. I suppose so. Don't we all fantasize most of the time?"

"I'm looking for special kinds of fantasy, honey. When did you first see that city that Tony painted?"

He pounded at her and made her remember. For the next two hours he kept at it with her. The painting, the phone call that she made and answered, the spilled wine. Dorothy was haggard-looking when Joanne jumped up and cried, "Mr. Davenport, stop it! You have to stop and leave her alone. Why are you doing this to her?"

Davenport seemed to collapse in his chair, his face was gray with fatigue, and the sparkle that had lighted his eyes was gone, leaving them pale.

"Why?" he repeated faintly. "I'm tired, hiding my fear hardly at all. We scratch about in the ashes of great men, picking their bones dry and clean, stripping all their ideas, their genius from them, pretending that we're onto something new, something that explains a little more to us. But we're not. And whatever it is that they already found out is only ashes and bones. Sometimes a genius just seems to step right over everything we know, everything he's known, and there is a new vista opened before our eyes. But not often. By God, it's rare. Sometimes an artist, or a poet, does the same thing, blindly striking out to find something that is so new, so breathtaking, so beautiful, or frightful, that it awes us and whether we want to or not we've got to go where the vision takes us. Most of the time we grovel in the ashes and cry in the night when our body sleeps and our soul weeps fearing the new day. It's always the same fear: Is it real? Is there meaning? Does it, any of it, matter? Ashes in our past, ashes in our future? Why? That's all that science is about, philosophy, religion, art. They're all asking the same question. Is it real, any of it?" He looked at Dorothy's pale face and touched her cheek lightly. "I'm sorry, my dear. But you see, you scare the living hell out of me. You're asking too, and my God, I'm afraid that you're going to get answers."

He turned and left them, an old man with slumping shoulders, weariness making his feet drag, his hands hanging limply at his sides.

"I'd better see that he gets home all right," Tony said. He looked at Joanne and then to Dorothy. "Will you two be all right?"

Joanne nodded and her stepmother hardly seemed to hear him. He hesitated another moment, then hurried after Perry Davenport.

"Dorothy, can I get you something? Are you all right?" Joanne reached over the table to touch Dorothy's hand. It was cold. She shook it and her stepmother seemed to rouse from a trancelike state and look at her. "Dorothy, I'm so afraid. I . . ." She burst into tears and, sobbing, let herself be held tightly in Dorothy's arms. After what seemed like a long time her sobs stopped and she could hear the murmuring voice, the comforting words, and she felt secure, and even loved. She pushed herself away and wiped her eyes with the back of her hand. Dorothy produced a tissue and Joanne blew her nose. "I'm a big help," she said hoarsely. "I wanted to do something for you and instead I cried like a baby."

"Honey, you did something for me. Believe me, you

did." Dorothy kissed her forehead and put her arm about the girl's shoulders. "Just rest a minute. It's been a hard weekend, hasn't it? What time is your plane?"

Joanne sighed and pulled away again. "I'm not going. How can I go away right now?"

"But your school . . . ?"

"Oh, I could stay away a month and not miss a thing except some girls' room gossip."

"I was afraid that you'd got tied up with Cramer. You know that you asked Tony Freemac to come over this afternoon?" Dorothy accepted the steaming glass from Gary and sipped the Tom Collins he had made for her.

"We worked earlier. Then I talked to a detective at the police station." Gary had his back turned, mixing his own martini then.

"Detective? Are you serious?"

"Of course. Someone must be planning a robbery or something. Probably quite by accident your double was found, and someone decided it was too good a chance to pass up. This woman will come in when you are out and clean out your jewelry, silverware, everything they can get away with. . . ." He stopped. Dorothy made a strangled noise. He turned and saw that she was laughing hysterically.

She felt as if she were far off watching it all, unable to intervene, unable to make the woman stop laughing, to make the man stop pouting like a baby whose rattle had been taken away. She watched and listened when Dorothy finally gasped, "And they believed this? The police believed someone is planning a robbery?"

"It was their idea." Gary took her hand and rubbed it gently. "Honey, this really worries me, the way you are taking all this."

She laughed harder. After a moment she began to calm down again and presently she asked quietly, "Gary, the other night. The first time. . . . I *was* on the beach."

He shook his head. "I saw you, darling. You were dreaming. You know I wouldn't lie to you. No one could deceive me into believing someone else was you. I went to the bedroom for my trunks, and to see if you were awake. You weren't. You had fallen asleep with your book across your legs. Your gown strap was down. I kissed the little mole by your right nipple. In God's name, how much more would it take to convince me that it was you asleep on that bed? What earthly reason would I have to lie to you about that? I love you, Dorothy."

She stood up and let him hold her. "Gary, I am so frightened. I believe you, all of it. But that wasn't me. I heard men talking. . . ."

"I'm frightened, too, darling. Not by what seems to have happened. I think you dreamed a very vivid dream. I'm frightened because you can't seem to distinguish between the two. I don't want you to mention that incident to the police at all, honey. I simply told them that when you were meeting Joanne's plane, someone else was impersonating you at Davenport's house. And again last night, when you were entertaining a guest with me, someone else was with Jo and Freemac pretending to be you."

She sighed. "You don't want me to talk about last night, Gary. You see, I have memories of being here, and of being with Jo and Tony." She looked at the table where she had knocked over her sherry. She touched the spot, looking for a sign of the spilled wine. It had been cleaned up. "And of the two, the other one seems more real."

Gary caught her shoulders and shook her hard. "Stop this! Did you let them talk to you this morning? Did Jo and Freemac convince you that you were with them?"

"No. Let go of me. You're hurting me."

He released her abruptly. His voice was harsh, almost unrecognizable. "You do need a doctor. You hear scraps of talk and weave them into a whole and think it actually happened to you. I shouldn't have given you that sleeping pill last night. It made you too receptive to suggestion. You heard that crazy kid and during the night you let bits and pieces of his story become real to you so that now you don't know what is real and what isn't. Who knows anything about him? He could be behind all this."

There was a tap on the door and they both turned to see Joanne. "Tony is here, Dad. You told him to come over at four, remember?"

Gary nodded. "Tell him to come on in. Why don't you go get some rest," he said to Dorothy.

"I'd rather stay and listen."

Gary shrugged and began to mix a new drink. Tony paused at the door, glanced from Gary to Dorothy's pale face, then to Joanne, who lifted her shoulders in an "I don't know," manner. "Suit yourself," Gary said. He faced Tony then. "I called the police about this impersonation business, and someone will be over at Davenport's tomorrow to talk to you. They think a robbery is the motive, and I'm inclined to go along with that."

Tony sat down and studied him as he spoke. Gary's voice became crisper. "All you should tell them is that a woman that you thought was Dorothy arrived over there and spent an hour or so with you and Joanne. The three of you came back here and you don't know what became of her. Dorothy was here when you arrived. Is that clear?"

"And that there really is a Santa Claus, and the Easter Bunny does bring the eggs."

"And what are my instructions?" Joanne asked angrily.

"You won't be here. You're a minor and I won't have them questioning you at all. You'll be at home with your mother."

"No I won't. I'm staying for the rest of the week."

"We'll talk about that later," Gary said. He turned again to Tony. "What could you add to what I just outlined that would do anything but confuse the whole issue?"

"And if it is already confused, we're to pretend it isn't. Is that it?" Tony glanced at his watch. "Mr. Davenport would like to talk to you sometime this afternoon," he said. "Are you going to give him a story too?"

"He's not mixed up in this," Gary said. "The police don't want to talk to him."

"But if there is a robbery planned, it might be his house that's being cased," Joanne said, too sweetly. "After all, the impostor did show up there twice now."

"Jo, I told you to keep out of this. If you interrupt again, I'll send you to your room."

"Don't you see, Daddy, that we can't tell your lies? It would show and they'd think we're all in a crazy conspiracy together. And if we tell them the truth, they'll want to send us all to the funny farm." Joanne caught a warning gesture from Dorothy and she subsided, sinking down into a chair that was about three sizes too big for her, making her look very tiny, very young.

"How much of this does Davenport know?" Gary asked Dorothy.

"Everything. He was over here earlier. I told him everything. He is mixed up in it, Gary. He's one of the witnesses, after all."

"I want him kept out of it," Gary said. "That's all we need to blow this into a big publicity splash."

"He said that he wants to talk to you about Amory Brock," Tony said.

Gary stared at him, then turned to stare at Dorothy. "Did he say anything else?" he asked after a long pause.

"No. He wants you to call him. That's all."

Gary nodded. He finished his drink and returned to the bar. He poured Scotch into his glass and drank it, then added more and squirted seltzer into it this time. Finally he said, "So there is a Brock?" Suddenly he spun around and shouted at Dorothy, "If you know something, why don't you just come out with it? Why all this hocus pocus? Who is Brock? Where does he fit in this business? What do you know?"

Very quietly Dorothy said, "I've told you everything I know."

"I don't believe you."

"I know."

Joanne and Tony were stretched out in the late afternoon sun. "Why is Dad reacting so violently?" she asked.

"Since I don't know how he usually reacts, I don't have much to go on."

"Cool, very cool. In charge. Controlled. Not afraid of something new and different."

"Unhuh. New and different within certain boundaries. New and different applications of the same old things."

"I suppose so," Jo said, thinking about it. "Like this thing that Dorothy calls the plastic abyss. Two old ideas put together in a new way. And you think that what's happening is something really new?"

Tony sat up. He let sand run through his fingers and watched it build, then fall again. "Jo, I think that what's happening is enough to shake every idea we've ever had about the universe right down to its core."

"Remember what Dorothy said about poltergeists? We stop hearing about it and then simply forget the whole thing. Isn't this like that?"

"I don't know. Davenport doesn't seem to think so." He smoothed the sand again and added, "Don't ask me these things. I'm not a scientist. I'm just a bum who dabbles with paint." He was thinking about something else Davenport had said to him: "You and the girl, you don't have anything at stake in all this. You're not threatened by a shake-up of reality. You don't know where it's at now, so why would it concern you to have it shift? But the others? Hazlett, Cramer, people like them, maybe even me, we've got a stake, we've built our lives on this one foundation and if you shake it too hard we might fall off and not land pretty."

"I'm ashamed of my father," Joanne said in a low voice. "You know that he's calling the police back and telling them that he made a mistake about Dorothy's being home all evening? He'll make Dr. Cramer back him up."

"Yeah. Can't say that I blame him too much. It was a dumb thing for him to do in the first place without more information than he had."

"Oh, he had it, but he wouldn't let himself see it."

"That's what I mean."

Dorothy and Gary stood at the porch door and looked at the two nearly naked bodies. "Isn't he a little old for her?" Gary asked.

"I don't know. Last week I would have said probably, but now, I just don't know. She's changed a lot in these two days."

"Dorothy, I'm sorry for that scene in the study. Davenport's due any second now, and I'd like for you to be in on it."

She nodded. "In a funny way I think yours is the most rational attitude of anyone mixed up in this. Those two out there simply accept. 'So there are two of her. How interesting, a little frightening, of course, but mostly just very curious.' And my own attitude. I'm afraid, but mostly curious, I think. I keep wondering if there is another me right now doing something somewhere else with someone else."

"Dorothy, don't. Let's not talk about this now. I can't accept it. There has to be an explanation. We'll find it."

"I know, dear. And that's comforting. You go right along with the statement: 'I think; therefore I am,' and I'm reduced to, I think I am. It's nice to have such certainty nearby." He drew her closer to him and she rested her head on his shoulder comfortably. "We're a nice pair. Other couples argue about religion or politics, so it's all right if we argue about what's real and unreal."

He squeezed her shoulder, too hard, but she didn't pull away. It was good to be hurt, to feel flesh and blood fingers on her flesh, to know that she was there, that he was there.

Perry Davenport arrived at six, accepted a shot of bourbon and a glass of ice water, and demanded that Joanne and Tony be permitted to sit in on the talk.

Gary didn't argue with him. When they had all gathered, Davenport said, "I want to tell you about the first government contract I ever got, Gary. I don't think you know the story, do you?"

Gary shook his head and the old man settled back in his chair and said, "It was early in the war, 'forty-two, and plastics was a new thing. We were all just beginning to get a whiff of the potentials at that time. Me and Pinelli worked twelve, fifteen, eighteen hours a day back then, just the two of us with a plant that was an old kitchen in a shed. All we had to our names, that shed, our ideas, and maybe five hundred dollars between us. We came up with Mirfab. And no one in Washington would talk to us. No one anywhere would talk to us. So I got me a torch and a piece of Mirfab about the size of a card-table top and I busted right into the middle of a fancy lunch where members of the Defense Department and a smattering of generals were bending their elbows. I busted in with that torch blazing full strength at that sample of plastic. They sat up, you bet your bottom dollar they did, and they listened. There was a pink-faced kid there. They'd got him fresh out of law school, put a uniform on him and taught him how to salute and called him lieutenant. Amory Brock. Lieutenant Amory Brock. We got to be buddies right quick, the young looie and me. He spent money on me like he owned the patent on it. And six months later Mirfab was being used in cockpits, on ships, seat coverings of jeeps. You name it, they had it. But none of it's ever been used in civilian life. You see? They own it for all practical purposes. Today they're using it on astronauts' suits, I hear."

He sipped his bourbon and looked at Gary thoughtfully. "I never went after another government contract," he said. "Lieutenant Brock rose to captain, then major, and now I hear he's a light colonel."

"But, the Defense Department does use a lot of our products," Gary said. "Corfloor, for example."

Davenport shook his head. "You don't seem to get the point, boy. Corfloor ain't ours no more. Mirfab ain't ours."

"Can they do that? Just take what you invent and keep it?" Joanne's voice was awed and indignant.

"Honey, what happens is this. We file for a patent, and they scan each and every patent application that goes in. Some of 'em get hauled out and stamped with a big red, S.O.—security order. It goes into a special envelope that is sealed, and the applicant gets a letter advising him that the Department of Defense, or the Army, or Navy, or whatever, has asked for a special hearing on that particular patent, that they foresee possible advantages in acquiring it for their forces, or something to that effect. A hand-picked board meets to consider those cases and if the decision goes in favor of the government, then you can go whistle up a stump. They can take it. They can sit on it, use it, contract for its manufacture, do whatever they want with it, and you're out of the picture. Oh, they have to pay. Eminent domain laws force them to pay the original applicant, but after that, he's off on the sideline somewheres wondering what happened."

Gary shrugged. "You can't have someone come up with a pocket-sized atom bomb and not be able to haul it out of the public files. National security demands such a law."

"Mebbe. Me, all I know is that Mirfab is not used for one goddam single civilian need. It should be on the walls of every schoolroom, should be in every home, in automobiles. It ain't. The Defense Department is a jealous mistress. It protects and keeps its own. Pinelli's been so careful this time. He made his first patent application five years ago on this stuff. We haven't named it, haven't given it special attention. Mixed up the patent application with a passel of others, and so far, we've not got that damned letter from Brock. But now . . . I don't know." He looked fondly at Dorothy. "You didn't pull that name out of thin air, honey. No sir, you did not. Brock is a name that marches through my nightmares."

Gary stood up and paced as he spoke. He seemed suddenly too restless to remain quiet. "You can't control what happens to what you invent. You put it out on the market and you don't know what people will use it for. You know what you intended, and that's all. If they decide that it has potential as a weapon, you can't help that."

"Right, but the point is that I want it for civilian use this time. I don't want to introduce it until we have it perfected as a building material to the point where it can be installed by any idiot who is pointed in the right direction. We are making it more and more simple, not more complicated. We want it to be used for buildings and energy to run those buildings, to light them and heat them and cool them. To run appliances in them. We won't let go until we have it worked down to such a fine point that any housewife will be able to go into a five and dime and order it by the yard and stick it on her house top with a tube of airplane glue."

"That plan won't necessarily be jeopardized," Gary said, but Davenport cut him off curtly.

"If this gets the S.O. stuck on it, we'll never see it again. Six months, maybe less than that, we'll be ready to put it out, and once the public gets its hands on it, there won't be no way to pull it back in. Then anyone could duplicate it, but not yet. There are still snags, as you know, since you're so hot for government money to step up the research."

"But if there's a leak, it won't matter anyway. They'll know. We should take advantage of our position and . . ."

Davenport stood up, ignoring Gary altogether. He looked at Dorothy and said slowly, "I'm not certain that in this world the secret's out. I'm not sure at all."

The abyss yawned before Gary suddenly and he clutched the arms of his chair. He heard Tony Freemac ask, "What does that mean?" He paid little attention to anyone in the room but stared ahead, slightly downward. Where had it come from, how?

"I don't know," Davenport said. "If there were two Dorothys there were two universes operating side by side, overlapping maybe. Either that, or a woman was created out of nothing to vanish back into nothing. And that introduces too much chaos, too much caprice even for me to swallow."

Gary knew there was no hole before him, knew that the floor was there, chairs, the rug. He had only to put his foot out to feel the rug. Slide it out carefully, inch by inch, over the thick pile, feeling the resistance, another inch, another. . . Nothing. His foot slipped from the rug over the edge, and with a gasp he jerked back. He closed his eyes, refusing to look into the blackness. It was unmoving, sharply defined, an opening that led nowhere into nothing.

"You're not serious about the alternate universes," Tony said. "And none of us believes that a woman can be created out of nothing, a real flesh and blood woman. What's left?"

The old man looked at Tony for a long moment, then said slowly, "Suppose, for the sake of a bit of mental exercise only, you understand, that there are forces manipulating the universe. Not Good and Evil, God and the Devil, nothing so fancy, just forces. Maybe from their elevated viewpoints they could define good and evil, but all we can do is say that today's evil might be tomorrow's good, and vice versa. Let's say that their motives and goals are unknowable. Only their methods and some of their actions show, and from these we can deduce certain directions. One direction is toward change and the other is toward stasis. And as far back as we can trace any history, written or otherwise, we know that those two directions have been present. Push forward. Pull back. And that the struggle between them has produced friction, hatreds, wars, all the evil we know."

Gary could hardly hear the droning voice now. He had to concentrate on refilling the void that he knew was still before him. Recreate the rug, thread by thread, take it out to the other side, fill in flooring beneath it. . . . Not to see the rug, and the chairs, not to feel the solidity of the floor was insanity. To fear that the void was enlarging even for one second was to risk absolute loss of control. He felt a tremor in his arm and loosened his grasp on the chair arm, then clutched it harder; the thought of an expanding void chilled him. He had never experienced this emptiness before. Never had to create reality before. Why now? Could he change the reality as he created it? He felt dizzy. The rug. Make it take shape in the blackness.

"Conservatism versus liberalism," Tony said dryly. "Seems a pretty mundane explanation for any of this."

"The players are as trapped as the pieces," Dorothy said suddenly. "Like a real game where the pieces can be moved only in restricted ways. The players are forced to follow rules that bind them. They can't stop the game, there are too many elements involved now, and they can't end it. They keep introducing more pieces, not different, only more, and they bog down in the same morass of rules and limitations." She remembered a dream of the water beetle skimming the surface of the water and thinking that was the entire universe.

Davenport watched her closely, and when she stopped, looking dreamy-eyed and remote, he said,

"The Greeks thought man's fate was in the hands of the gods, and Shakespeare put it another way: All the world's a stage, and we play our parts as written, or get replaced. But what's backstage? Where are the gods located? Who wrote the script? If an intelligent knight tumbled from a chessboard, wouldn't he be startled to find that his small board was just a very small speck in the universe?"

"Poor knight," Dorothy said, still dreamily. "Taken from his box and used awhile, then returned, learning nothing, gaining nothing. Momentary pleasures, momentary pains, then the blackness of the box. Only the player grows with each game, becoming wiser and more skillful."

"But still a player bound by the rules, forced to obey certain laws," the old man said.

Tony realized that the old man was leading her on, trying to coax something out of her, watching her as attentively as a surgeon watches the incision he has opened. And Dorothy seemed far apart from them, not looking at any of them, answering the leading statements and questions automatically, without effort, without thought.

"But if the player wins enough games, he can alter the rules, he can write new ones. He moves into a different class, a new category."

"And the pieces? Can they change categories?"

"Not most of them. They're mindless, thoughtless, programmed to do certain things only. They can't change. Some of them, somehow, get glimpses of the universe beyond the playing board, and they are given the chance to move into it, to leave the smaller world for the larger one, if they dare. Most of them don't realize what it is they're being offered, and they are afraid. So they go back to sleep."

Gary realized with a start that he was no longer hearing Dorothy's voice, not with his ears. It was inside him, part of him, as if she were speaking to him alone in a secret way that only they understood. He couldn't listen to her now, he had to remake the room that he had lost. He couldn't tell if he had finished or not without opening his eyes, and he was afraid to. Desperately he visualized the area as it had to be and very reluctantly he looked. There was still one small patch of the blackness, and as he looked into it, he thought he could see an image forming there, a woman. . . . He shut his eyes.

"The worst part of it," Dorothy said, and suddenly her voice lost its dreamy sound, and was firm and controlled again, "is that we can't help each other. We are given the choice or not; like Calvin's predestination, you are formed in such a way that you will or won't be able to see beyond the board."

"That's a worse theory than the alternate universe," Tony said.

"I know," Davenport admitted. "It's sort of like putting the whole concept of God into the old, white-bearded gentleman who is omnipotent. Guts knowledge. A certain amount of information gets lost in translation."

"So how about an explanation that we can understand?"

"His impersonation theory," Davenport said, indicating Gary. He was sitting rigidly with his eyes closed. Davenport looked more closely at him, then said, "Gary, are you all right?"

Dorothy jumped up and ran across the room to his side. "Gary, what's wrong?"

He felt her hand on his arm and opened his eyes. The rug, chairs, solid flooring, a layer of smoke hanging in air. . . . "Nothing," he said. "Nothing. I was trying to think, that's all." He felt her hand, firm, real, fingers digging in, and he covered it with his hand. "I think we're all sharing a mass hallucination," he said. "Maybe we're all suffering from food poisoning. Something as simple as that."

"You saw it, something, didn't you?" Dorothy asked, her fingers on his arm digging in even harder.

"What? I saw what? Nothing."

Dorothy's hand loosened its grip and she moved away slowly. "I don't know," she said. "I don't know." She looked about her. "A poltergeist would be easier, wouldn't it? We could all disbelieve in it together. We could read books on it, call in investigators, rig cameras, laugh at it over drinks. But this. . . We can't name it, can't describe it, but we all know that something is happening, something that can't happen in the world we know." She half turned to the hallway. "Listen," she said. "There's someone going out through our French doors."

Tony was the first one in the hallway, with Joanne and Davenport close behind. Dorothy had moved aside, and Gary was still sitting in his chair. He remembered the way his foot had slipped off the rug, downward, like slipping off the edge of a cliff.

"Are you afraid to get up?" Dorothy asked.

They could hear Tony shouting, "Stop! Come back! We have to talk to you."

Gary stood up. The rug was solid. Keeping his eyes on Dorothy, he took a step, then another. The rug was solid, as was the floor beneath it.

"We could see anything there is to see from the patio," she said, starting toward the outer doors.

"No! No, let's just wait for them to come back." Gary took the final step and was clear of the space that had been taken over by the abyss. He turned to look at it. The rug was there, the chairs in place. It had been an hallucination.

Dorothy was walking toward the patio, and he followed her. The sun was low in the sky, blinding them momentarily. A bank of clouds was afire, shot through with scarlet, gold, orange. The ocean was smooth glass that reflected the gaudy sky, gold at the horizon, the gold narrowing, pointing to them like an arrow.

Dorothy smiled, staring at the golden avenue. Again.

"There's the old man," Gary said. He took a step past Dorothy and called out, "What was it?"

Davenport turned and came back from the sea wall to join them. "Well, you won't like this, Gary, but from all appearances, it was your wife." He studied Dorothy, with a faint smile on his face. Then he shook his head, but he said nothing more.

"I know where she'll go," Dorothy said, gazing at the golden boulevard. "Into the water." Like walking into a haze that hides what's on the other side of it. . . . Walking on the avenue, gently rolling green on either side, aware of the others on the sand, following, but afraid, floundering. Walking down the city streets, smiling now at other strollers, glancing back, back through the haze, pitying them on the sand, wet, clinging together, staring at the water. Laughing softly, with pity, with love.

"For God's sake, Dorothy! Snap out of it!" Gary shaking her.

"She walked right into the water."

"Not in it, on it."

"She vanished into the water! Just vanished. She didn't sink, or drown, or anything. She vanished!"

"Get the child a drink," Davenport said. "Something."

"A mass hallucination," Gary. Explaining, explaining, his voice insistent, persuasive. Gary, not believing a word until he uttered it aloud, then believing it to be gospel. We say what we want to hear, not what others want to hear, and when it pleases us, we call it truth.

Joanne, weeping almost in her efforts to understand what she was saying. "Walked on the water, not in it, on top of it." Weeping, listening to her words, not believing them, afraid not to say them because she feared the denial of what she had seen, needed to believe what her eyes saw.

"We never see what we think we do. It's a matter of training. We see lines, and we join them. We see

partial figures, and we complete them. We see random-
ness and we make it orderly. Our minds refuse chaos,
so we train our eyes and our brain to create order."
Tony, wondering what order of chaos his eyes were
reporting when they saw a woman walking on water.
What order of reason his brain could derive from
that, given time enough.

Dorothy on her knees by Davenport's chair saying,
"Drink this. I'll hold it." No memory of returning to
the study. No memory of sitting down, of seeing the
others find chairs and sit down. Joanne's shoes were
dry; she had changed clothes. Tony still wore his wet
things. Beyond them all the evening was growing
dark, twilight now. Half an hour or more, gone without a trace.

"I'll take him home," Tony said. "Jo, how about a
drive later?" She nodded and he walked out holding
Davenport's elbow.

Dorothy tried to talk to Gary about the city. "It's
as if all this is a curtain that can be drawn back to let
me see what's actually there." She waved her hand at
the room. "Not a curtain, but the idea of a curtain,
with depth, a substantial curtain deep enough to hold
everything we think is real. . . ."

He stood up and started to leave the room. "Not
tonight, Dorothy. Maybe never, but not now." His
voice was too controlled, and with his back to her
and his face hidden, she could tell nothing about him,
except that he was not going to listen to her, that he
would not talk about it. She watched him go silently.

There were fourteen guests at Perry Davenport's
party. "They hate you for the beard," Joanne whispered to Tony, after the dinner was over and every-
one was gathering in the improvised theater. "And me
because I'm too young to tell dirty stories to, and too
old not to understand them if they tell each other."

"Don't forget that I'm in the enemy's camp here,"

he said. "They recognize dimly that if I have a box, its shape is different from theirs, bigger maybe, but at least different."

"Box?"

"Sure. The limits of what you can do, how high you can grow, how far to the right or left you can step, how much deviation your brain is allowed before it comes to the edge. A bag. A box."

"Look at them. They're like dolls, all wound up with this program punched for tonight. Be polite, smile at the jokes of your equals, laugh at those of your superiors. Flirt, drink, make small talk. It's all so predictable, so horrible. And they don't know they are all pre-set."

"The box," Tony said. "Or, in your terms, a computer program. Anything not punched in can't be grasped, seen, understood, or even guessed at."

"Why don't you have one?"

"I guess I do, but it's different, gives me more leeway. Maybe that's the whole answer. We all have some blank tape, computer tape, and we fill it in as we choose. They've chosen that way. How will you fill yours in, little bit?"

But Joanne had become deadly serious. She glanced about the room: Gary talking in low tones to Dr. Cramer. "His would be very narrow and restricted, wouldn't it?" Joanne said, watching the thin face of the scientist as he spoke. "And Dad, is he programmed?" She nodded to herself and answered the question. "Of course. He has to win. He's programmed to win all the time, to see nothing but the small victory he's driving for. He never plans for more than whatever he's doing at the moment. He never seems to think of the past or beyond tomorrow. Only this one moment."

Davenport mounted the stage, and Tony said, "My cue. Wish me luck, little bit."

"I do."

"Ladies and gentlemen," the old man said, and there

was immediate silence in the room. "I have asked you tonight to bear with me and the rehearsal of the show that will be presented to our company in three weeks at the annual ball. Now, I know that this will bore every soul in this room with the exception of me, but since I am the boss of the company, and since this is important to me, I trust that you will all pay attention to my little skit. I would appreciate any suggestions you might have to make following this rehearsal. Please feel free to criticize, to suggest change, anything you feel might make a better presentation, without changing the content of what you are about to see."

The old man took a legal-sized sheet of paper from a folder and read from it: "In the year 1868, September 29, one Alexander Davenport was hanged by the neck until dead, having been convicted of the heinous crime of treason and espionage." He looked up from the paper. "Alexander Davenport, as you all know, was my grandfather. Unfortunately he was not a wealthy man, not an important man. The notation I read to you is the only mention of him the courthouse revealed. But he was a man, of flesh and blood, who left an heir, my father. And he was a man wrongfully hanged, wrongfully accused of a crime which he did not commit. Let the play begin."

He stepped aside and the curtain was drawn back to reveal the judge's chair, the chair of the accused, occupied by a bearded man and behind and to one side the shadow of a gallows.

"Guilty!" said a voice from behind stage. Tony stood up and faced the audience.

"Guilt implies a knowledge of what is true, and the truth is not yet known. How can you know what is true when your eyes see only what you will, when your ears hear only what you wish to hear, when your tongues speak only what you wish to be said. Does every man have the right to shape the truth into the likeness that is most pleasing to himself, altering all facts to conform to his needs . . . ?" Tony paused, as if

he had forgotten his lines. He closed his eyes and
groped behind himself for the edge of the desk, anything to hold. It lasted only a moment, then he opened
his eyes once more and looked at the audience. When
he spoke his voice was different, deeper, more com-
manding. He said, "You have gathered here to unveil
the truth. Let us proceed."

It proceeded backward, forward, sideways.

He was hanged.

He watched himself hanging.

He was found guilty.

He was found not guilty.

He was not tried at all.

He was married/not married.

His wife was pregnant/not pregnant.

The stage was a window looking out onto another
world, a world that shifted and changed and faded into
shadows to be replaced by another firmer world.
There were battles; there were cotton fields; there
were mountains and prairies, and oceans. There were
children playing, growing old, dying, turning to ashes,
blowing away. There were mammoth trees growing,
toppling, rotting, turning to ashes, blowing away. A
bearded man was hanged. The same man stood on the
ground and watched the hanging. The same man
walked past the scene oblivious of it altogether. He
grew young, lost his beard, became shrunken, pink-
cheeked, vanished into the womb of his mother, who
spun back in time and vanished. The bearded man
walked past, became stooped, his hair and beard
whitened, his skin darkened, his back bent, his legs
grew weak and wobbly. He walked to his deathbed
and died on it and turned to ashes and the ashes drifted
from the window and were lost.

Gary saw it and refused it. He closed his eyes and
waited until it was over.

Joanne saw it in fear and dread, but she watched it
through.

Perry Davenport saw it and his heart pounded,

blinding him with pain so that he could see no more.

Tony saw it, was in it, and he accepted it and moved with it.

Dorothy saw it.

Dr. Cramer saw nothing. Hank Pinelli saw and rejected it. Others saw something they didn't understand, saw and refused the vision, and forgot.

The curtain closed again and there was a moment's silence. Then applause. "Perry, it was marvelous! Who wrote it?"

"Mr. Davenport, you could put it on a commercial stage. . . ."

"I was so moved. Look, I've been weeping. . . ."

Joanne drew closer to Tony, who was pale. "My dear boy," Mrs. Jarvis was saying to him, "you made it come alive. You certainly must talk to my friend, Wallace Upton. The producer, you know. . . ."

Dorothy stood to one side and watched the others. She saw the pallor of Joanne's face and knew the girl had shared the experience; as had Tony, and Gary. Mr. Davenport was shaken and quiet now. Dorothy moved toward him, but there were five or six of his guests crowding about his chair and she was stopped. He looked at her and stood up. He pushed his way through the people between them and said to Dorothy, "What is the truth? How can we ever know?"

"I don't know. I think we all have to mold it with our own hands, shape it, work with it."

There was a sharp ring of a spoon on a wineglass and they turned to look again at the stage. Dr. Cramer was standing on it. "God damn it," Davenport said. "Where's Pinelli? Is he double-crossing me too now?"

"The second half of our show, ladies and gentlemen, a sneak preview, so to speak," Cramer announced.

He stepped aside and at the same time the muslin curtain again was pulled open. The scene was as it had been before, the desk, chair, and gallows. With a flicker of light the scene vanished to be replaced by a forest glen with three scantily dressed girls dancing before a man playing a flute. Someone in the audience laughed. Someone close to Dorothy muttered, "How the devil did he get those trees in here?" It seemed very real. Dorothy couldn't tell where the projectors were.

The dance ended to applause. The girls curtsied prettily, and the images vanished to reveal a rocket and a tank on the stage, each one in silhouette only, stark black against the paler darkness of the night outside. There was a flicker and the rocket became a massive oak tree, the tank became a hut; flicker, the rocket was a lighthouse, the tank a fishing boat on a sparkling ocean. Flicker, the rocket was a pillar of a large building, the tank an automobile parked before it.

It ended as suddenly as it started. A final flicker of light, the tank and rocket again revealed in black, then curtain. There was stunned silence afterward.

Hank Pinelli broke it. "You can't be serious, Gary. I told you that the sophisticated methods of detection wouldn't be fooled a minute. . . ."

Dorothy moved from the group toward the door. The voices sounded distant and faint. "We have a dozen devices that would penetrate your illusions," Pinelli was saying. "It's a childish trick, that's all."

She stepped outside on the porch. The breeze was strong now, and fresh smelling. In her mind she saw the stage again: the muslin curtains, which she pulled aside to reveal the dancing girls and the flute player, another curtain. She pulled it aside. And the tree and the fishing boat, and the building and automobile. All were cast aside. Then the rocket and tank. She hesitated a moment, then added them to the discarded images. Blackness now to be filled in. Illusion, reality, illusion, layer on layer to be stripped away, and when the final reality rested alone with no more illusion. . . Could man ever achieve that reality? She thought of it as a scale, a ladder with great open spaces between the rungs. The rungs were reality, the open spaces illusion to be filled in by the climber, and how he filled them in determined the next step. She could hear Gary's voice, although he was across the room, speaking in an insistent whisper to Pinelli and the old man.

"For God's sake, Pinelli, pay attention. You have to shift gears. You've been thinking of this stuff in one way for so long that you can't focus in on other applications. Think of a squadron of planes, all covered with your material, all projecting images of blue sky and clouds, or whatever is appropriate. No radar is going to show them. It's going to be absorbed and used by them."

Down the porch from Dorothy, Tony and Joanne were standing close together, Jo talking. "You just don't know what it's like. You go into the school, shapeless, unfinished, and they begin to fill you in, turn you into the sort of person they don't have to watch and wonder about. You're like a sponge that soaks everything up without discrimination and when you're done, you're one of them. I have to get out of it, far away from it. I just have to. I don't know what I am, who I am, why, anything."

Back to the inside, listening to the sharp voice of Perry Davenport, "You're nothing, Gary, another hand on a body that can be lopped off any time. There's only two in the whole company that matter and they're Hank and me. We're the two-headed monster that runs it all, and now and again we pick up a new hand that's fancy, or that can write pretty letters, or, like you, that has good connections and looks good in the journals, but we can lop it back off if it begins scratching where we don't itch."

Dorothy could make out the next step now. She hesitated, but only a moment, because she knew that the struggle wouldn't end with it, that it would be intensified and more painful, but the pleasures and joys would also be greater. She could see the party now, all of it, all the guests, could hear all of their conversations at once and keep them separated. She could see the woman they called Dorothy standing alone on the porch, apart from the others, staring out at the dark sea where phosphorescent swells rolled toward the shore like blue shadows, to rise into blue-white breakers shooting out in both directions with crashing sounds.

She turned her attention to Joanne and the girl said to Tony, "Have you swum at night when the sea is calm like this? There are millions of dinoflagellates that glow. They coat your arms and legs and it is ghostly and beautiful."

She watched them walk hand in hand down the beach away from the lights and shed their clothes, and walk out into the glowing surf.

Gary searched for Dorothy and finally found her on the porch. "Let's go," he said.

"Is something wrong?"

"I'll let you know tomorrow. I think the old man just canned me."

Legs doing a scissors kick in the water were like white wings opening and closing, leaving diaphanous streamers behind. Tony watched them and he felt that something had happened to him that night that would change his future, as if he had stepped from one world into another without noticing the threshold. He had experienced a hanging, birth, death, love, and agony; he knew that each experience had been true and real, each had marked him in a way that vicarious experience could not. He felt at once exhilarated and awed by the new sense of power he felt he had. He wanted daylight to hurry so he could get to his oils. With a laugh, he pulled Joanne to him and kissed her hard and they both sank, sputtering and laughing, in the quiet water.

Hank Pinelli handed the old man his bourbon and water and sat down heavily. "I don't know how long we can keep it now," he said. "We tried. By God, we gave it a good try."

The old man swallowed half his drink without answering. Then he looked at his friend and it seemed to him later that everything blurred at that moment, that what had been separated and lonely became whole and peaceful. When he spoke, his face was serene and his voice firm. "We'll keep it, Hank. We're carving a future that's going to be different, and we're still carving. We're not out yet."

The new Player touched each of her pieces lovingly and watched them go their separate ways. She would try to make them see glimpses of the next step, and those who were ready for it would see and take the step, and she would try to see what her own next step was to be, and who her adversaries were. And one day, or year, or millennium, she would finally understand the goals and the reasons. There was time. She could wait and play out the present game and join in the new ones where they started. She would initiate her own games. There was time.

Stranger In the House

Robert drove slowly up the driveway to the monster of a house, grinning at it happily. Mandy laughed aloud. The house was a joke played on a dignified dowager, after all. It was a three-story mixture of fieldstone and wide siding with a porch that ran around three sides of it. The original building had been constructed in 1820, it was thought, and the upper floors had been added later. There were two-story-high columns dwarfing the double front doors; windows on the first floor bowed outward in pairs symmetrically spaced, and the windows above had been lined up with them. But on the third floor it looked as if the builder had fallen heir to an assortment of windows of which no two were alike in size, shape, or operation. Some opened outward, others raised from the bottom up, some were louvered, there was even a pair of skinny French windows. A funny house, for God's sake, Robert thought. On the back seat the two-part sign shifted, and the chain connecting the top to the bottom jiggled. The sign read: Phillips Insurance Agency, in colonial motif; the bottom half was starkly modern: Amanda Fashions. This weekend he would hang the sign, making the move official even if the movers weren't due for six more days.

Robert parked the car around at the back of the house. He was looking past the yard to the woods beyond. "You know, sometimes it takes something awfully big to make you open your eyes and see where you are. The heart attack did it, didn't it?"

Mandy turned to him quickly, and he smiled as her gaze searched his face. They both knew that she couldn't help it; after his heart attack of almost two years ago, she found herself studying him intently like that at the slightest provocation.

"I mean pulling out of the city like this. A country house, for heaven's sake. Us in a country house!"

"It does seem out of character. It will take getting used to, I suppose. Twenty-two years in various apartments. . ." Mandy laughed again, and suddenly she flung open her car door and was out and running lightly toward the back door of the house. Robert followed more slowly, enjoying watching her. Mandy was small and quick, with a fluidity of motion that was like liquid. She had very short dark hair, untouched yet by gray, black eyes that snapped and gleamed and teared easily, annoying for her, but keeping them sparkling and alive looking. She was all energy and tight muscles inclining toward thinness, which she fought with a diet that would have had Robert back in the hospital within a week.

Mandy hummed as she worked in the house, waiting for the neighborhood boy to arrive to help her sort junk that was piled to the ceiling in the garage. Once she looked out the window and saw Robert standing with two men in dungarees who were cleaning out the brook and repairing the dam that made a lake on the property. She watched them for several minutes, Robert so straight and Brooks Brotherish, so out of place here. She would buy corduroys for him, maybe even denims. She tried to visualize him in denims and failed. The boy arrived then.

Late Saturday night she and Robert agreed that
moving was hard work. "You go on up and take a
bath while I load the dishwasher," Mandy said, when
Robert yawned for the third time. "I'll be up in a
couple of minutes." He kissed her right eye without
argument and left her, yawning again. She knew that
she had wanted to be alone, tired, content in the lovely
house. She wanted to touch the woodwork, run her
hand over the cabinets, just gloat over it. Why hadn't
either of them ever brought up the possibility of moving from the city? It seemed such a natural thing for
them to do. She hadn't dreamed that Robert would
be willing to move, and probably he had thought the
same about her. If he had been able to peek inside her
just once during those years, he would have known
how she had yearned for the country, for a yard and
woods and green things growing. She stopped scrap-
ing the dishes and stared ahead for a moment, then
continued briskly. There were always things about
people that never came out unless they were asked
point blank. Why should either of them have guessed?

But it didn't matter now. They were here and loved
it. Their twenty-year-old daughter Tippy loved it,
and Laura would come around once she saw it, although she was very disapproving from a distance.
She was studying art in Paris. Tippy was a math
major at London University. If only they had had
such a place while they were both children at home,
Mandy thought regretfully. "Cut it out!" she said to
herself sharply then and clicked off the kitchen light.
The living room lamps were still on. It was the only
other room downstairs that was even partially fur-
nished. She stood in the doorway studying the green
frosty-looking draperies, the gold and amber chairs
and couch, and she nodded approvingly.

She swayed suddenly and reached out for support,
and her hand found nothing to grasp. She closed her
eyes hard. The room had become different momentarily, ugly, too garish and bright, shaped weirdly with

abrasive angles, oppressively hot and airless. She opened her eyes again and looked about, but the room was completely normal. She felt curiously lightheaded. Whatever it had been, the attack was over. Indigestion? It had been so fleeting, long enough to close her eyes and open them again. Two seconds perhaps. She left the room and went to the wall panel of switches that controlled all the lights in the downstairs rooms. She switched off the lights, and with the darkness, she was enveloped in terror. Nothing else, simply terror. She jabbed at the switches again, and with the return of light, her moment of fear was gone. She laughed weakly, but when she turned off the lights again, she was careful to leave the hall lights on.

Robert was already asleep when she tiptoed through the bedroom. She relaxed in a tub of hot water and read a chapter in the book he had left by the tub. *Scandinavian Film Making.* Well, he would have space now for a darkroom, and a projection room, and his collection of 8 mm. films. . . .

Robert groaned, a long, loud, wordless sound of pain, or protest, and Mandy dropped the book. She was out of the bath and standing by the bed with her robe around her dripping body without awareness of having moved. He was sleeping peacefully now. A dream? She bit her lip hard, wanting to wake him, to make certain he was all right, not willing to disturb him. . . . She became chilled then and walked slowly back to the bathroom and finished drying herself. She saw the book in the tub and fished it out. It was ruined. She dropped it into the waste basket, and then got into bed beside Robert, snuggling very close to him. She left the bathroom light on, and the door partially open.

The next morning Robert went down to the village for a newspaper while she made breakfast. While they ate they talked about the house. "Why didn't anyone live in it for the past thirty years?" Mandy asked.

"People have put thousands of dollars in improvements in it, and yet none of them stayed. Why?"

"Mostly because of the thousands of dollars' worth of improvements. The last guy went stone broke. If it weren't for our combined businesses being relocated in the house, we couldn't afford the upkeep on it either, honey. For us it'll be cheaper than the offices in town, but for a private family? Uh-huh." He turned to the financial page then, but looked up and said, "Oh, Gus Farley said his kid got sick here yesterday. Did he eat anything?" She shook her head. "Well, Gus said the boy won't work here this summer, after all. He shouldn't have said he could. He's booked solid already."

"If we can't get any local help, we'll be in real trouble," Mandy said slowly. "We can't run a house like this by ourselves."

"I'll get a riding mower and cut the grass myself."

"If you get a go-go mower, I'll cut the damned grass," Mandy said quickly.

On Monday Mandy's ad in the village weekly was answered. "Ellen Turnbull," she said excitedly, "would like an interview on Thursday. She can start immediately."

"If she can start Thursday, let her. My God! I was dreading moving without someone to help out."

"Yeah," Mandy said. "Me too. One week to go, darling, and the worst part will be over. Then all we'll have to do is find everything again."

The Groth stirred slowly with great pain and inspected the door seal when its alarm pulsated relentlessly, signaling an entry had been made. They had returned again. Every movement it made was tortuous, and it wanted only to be left alone now to die without further effort. It returned to its tank bed, a semi-rigid material that yielded to the Groth's mass, closed itself, and released a spray that soothed, but no longer healed the occupant. The Groth lapsed into an uneasy sleep once more.

The room beneath the house was filled with instruments: recording devices, a screen that was blank then, listening devices, a powerful transmitter that was hooked into a translator and coder. There was a tank filled with a murky thick olat culture—the Groth food bank—and equipment that altered the atmosphere within the sealed room; the room was almost dark, like a room seen at the last light of dusk. The temperature was held at a constant, comfortable 40° F. The Groth lacked nothing to make life comfortable during its stay on Earth, nothing but the companionship of its lifemate, long since dead now. Also, the Groth was dying, and knew that the mission to Earth was a failure, and the taste of failure was bitter. It slept restlessly, dreaming of the seas on Gron where the young sported, and in the dream it was a young Groth, diving deep to catch the lifemate that teased and eluded it again and again. The seas were alive with olat, and there were no dangerous forms, and so life there was safe and happy. Its dreams repeatedly took it to the seas of Gron, and each time it awoke, the awakening was more painful and distressing.

This day it returned to consciousness with the memory of noises in the building above it, and with a resolve that one last effort had to be made. Arising from the moist bed dulled the bright glow of the resolution, and the hope of fulfilling the mission became once more the distant unattainable goal that the Groth knew it to be. The hope that had roused it returned to the seas of sleep while the Groth started the routine that it knew must be done.

It drew off its daily ration of olat, measured the acidity of the culture, added liquid to replace what it had taken, and closed the tank again. It sucked in the olat and then checked the life systems that kept the bed spray at the correct concentration of sulphuric acid, and the air at the correct mixture of oxygen, sulphuric acid, nitrogen, and trace elements. The pressure was holding at a constant nine pounds per square inch, and that was satisfactory. After the inspection of the systems, the Groth turned to the information gathering equipment and began feeding the data into the translator and coder. It no longer paid much attention to the data, no longer was interested in the storms of the western oceans, and the wars of the entire globe that broke out here and there like fires spotting a dry mountain slope. Measurements were being made automatically by the equipment the pair of Groth had installed during the first years of their stay on Earth; all aspects of Earthmen endeavors were being watched and recorded: rainfall, wind velocities, temperatures, population changes, mining operations, construction projects, constant wars, the change in design in automotive and aircraft industries, atomic energy research, the advancing space efforts. . . . Every spoken language of Earth had been thoroughly analyzed by them, and fed into the computer so that there could be communication when the time came. University classes were monitored daily, newspapers scanned, radio and television programs recorded for analysis, churches surveyed and the various faiths sorted one from another, cross-indexed and cross-filed in the computer, interwoven with myths and history, so that a picture would emerge when the right Groth inspected the data and studied it thoroughly.

But only nine years after their arrival, the lifemate had been injured. Unable to believe the extent of the economic depression that plunged the planet into despair, threatening war, and the ruin of the timetable of forecasts, the lifemate had gone out to inspect personally some of the unbelievable events flickering dimly on the television screen. While the lifemate was flying over the incredible dust bowl area of the southern region, a tornado, a storm system unknown to the Groth, had swept out of nowhere, caught the tiny craft in its vortex, and smashed it to ground miles

away. The terrible heat, the sun's rays, and the driving
dust tormented the lifemate, desperately making re-
pairs on the craft. By the time it was operable again,
the lifemate had been mortally burned. When the
Groth back in the vlen heard the agony being broadcast unguardedly, it was too late to save the lifemate.
The injured Groth returned on automatic controls.
It was not able to maintain mind shielding then, and
the broadcast of pain had gone out into the air, into
the house above the vlen, and one of the Earthmen,
a female, had died, and two more had been driven
insane.

The Groth had known then that it had to move the
vlen away from the fragile Earthmen, who proved so
susceptible to its thoughts, and the following year it
had started to carry out the planned move, when mys-
teriously, the house was emptied. The Groth waited
for developments. When new Earthmen moved in
above it, again it contemplated moving. It was the
summer season of the planet, however, and the Groth
knew the heat would weaken it, making the move
more dangerous and arduous than if it waited for cold
weather to begin. It settled in and shut down its shield
very tight, and simply monitored its electronic devices.
But the new Earthmen, child Earthmen, also wished to
avoid the heat, and they played in the basement of the
building, very close to the vlen. And one of the child
Earthmen reached out with mental fingers he didn't
know he possessed, and he felt the stranger nearby.
The child Earthman screamed in terror. The Groth
staggered back from the momentary, unplanned contact, shaken by the alien mind, sickened by the images
felt through it, in agony when its own nerves responded to the glare of light seen by the child. Later
the same night, the Groth was pulled from a deep
sleep into full wakefulness by the sudden intrusion of
an unprotected mind probing into his. The Earthman
child screamed in the Groth's head, and both were
sickened by the unshielded, uncensored contact. The

Earthman child couldn't break the contact; there was a complete lack of control, and by the time the Groth disentangled the thoughts that were its own from those that were alien, the Earthman child was seriously ill, with a raging fever. He died within the hour.

The Groth mourned the death of the Earthman child, blaming itself for the accident, even though the child had found the way to the Groth unaided. It probed gently into the mind of the sole remaining Earthman in the house above it and the Earthman became paralyzed with shock and fear. The Groth knew then that it could never again touch the mind of one of the Earthmen, and it again prepared to move to a totally uninhabited region, far north of the present location of the vlen.

The Groth pulled its thoughts from the past to the present. There were the simple, basic problems now to settle. Earthpeople were once more in the building above it. It was being offered one last chance to salvage the mission that was of paramount importance. With the assistance of one of the Earthpeople, it might still be saved. All summer and fall it had lain on the bed, semi-aware only; it awoke each day to maintain the equipment, then lapsed back into the dream life of its youth. Winter came and the Groth knew that its own death was not far away. Its breathing was shallow and painful, unsatisfying, and the attacks of dizziness that now came to it lasted longer and were more confusing. Determinedly it again forced the past away, and it wondered if it mattered now that there were again Earthpeople within reach. It didn't know if it had enough strength remaining to it to make an attempt worthwhile now. The Groth knew that once it had accepted failure, its last acts would be of destruction. All traces of the orbiting satellite, of the spaceship on Earth, of the vlen under the building, and finally of itself had to be obliterated completely once it accepted failure.

Very tentatively it reached out and found the Earthman female, and both recoiled from the touch. It touched the male later, and left even more hastily. The male was weakened by a heart injury. He must never be touched again. The Groth mused about the female, and knew it would try again to contact her.

By Thursday Mandy felt as though she had been running a month. She drove to the house in the country through a hard rain, but once inside the rain and wind seemed far removed. Straightening from removing her boots at the back entry, she saw an oil smear on the floor, half under the basement door. She opened the door and looked at it closer. Who could have dropped oil there? She started to touch the shiny smear, but drew back her hand quickly and closed the door again. She glanced at the phone, then tried it, but without hope of finding it operating yet. They said in the afternoon. It was eleven then; Mrs. Turnbull was due at one. There was time to measure the third-floor windows and try to plan the rooms there.

The third floor had five small rooms in a row, all roughly finished: servants' rooms probably. There was also a very large L-shaped room. Room for the sewing machines and cutting tables, for bolts of materials, and accessories, shelves, work tables, everything. Besides, there was the rest of the third floor unfinished, but with rough flooring laid, and with windows. Surveying it, she gloated again over the space, well lighted, clean, warm, airy. . . . And absolutely quiet.

She stopped moving about the room and listened. The quiet was so profound that she wished she had brought a radio with her, or that they were just a little closer to a highway, or a neighborhood playground. Or something. The house seemed to be holding its breath.

She frowned angrily. She never had been timid, or afraid of being alone, or spooky. And there was nothing about the house that was frightening. It was a friendly house, a welcoming house. She finished measuring the windows quickly, whistling between her teeth as she worked.

At twelve-thirty she made coffee and opened a can of soup for her lunch. The rain was driving against the house furiously now. She still didn't want to go out to the car to bring in curtains.

Mrs. Turnbull showed up as Mandy was washing her dishes. Mrs. Turnbull was about fifty, with obviously dyed red hair, the suspicion of a mustache that required frequent shavings, and legs like a football player. She had very blue eyes that darted about in suspicious glances all the time she talked with Mandy.

"You Missus Phillips? I'm Ellen Turnbull. Gus Farley says you're looking for a woman to do for you? Can't sleep in, though. Got a boy in high school, and a girl with a baby at home. Can't be off nighttimes." Within fifteen minutes Mandy had hired her.

"Can you start tomorrow?" Mandy asked.

"Be here at nine. Do I get a key?"

"A key? Of course. But I'll have to have an extra one made. . . ."

"Give it to me and I'll do that while you're still here. You won't be here by nine tomorrow will you? When are the movers due?"

"At one," Mandy said. Silently she searched her bag for her key and handed it to the red-haired woman. Perhaps the hair wasn't dyed, she thought suddenly.

After Mrs. Turnbull left with her key Mandy realized that she had not even asked for references. She knew she wouldn't ask for references, either. Not from her. Her presence was all the reference she needed. Mandy laughed suddenly and when she lifted the phone, the line was connected. Gaily she dialed Robert's office number, and she was humming as she waited for his answer.

Robert agreed that she had done right to follow her instincts about Mrs. Turnbull. "I'll make discreet inquiries about her in the village," he said. "She sounds like a doll. Why don't you ask if her son can take on the yard when she comes back?"

Mandy hung up, still grinning, and decided to bring in the curtains and get them hung while she waited for the return of her new housekeeper. She slipped on her coat and made a dash for the car. The rain was not driving in an angle now but was still coming down hard and very steadily. She covered the drapes carefully with sheets and ran back to the protection of the back stoop, and she found that she had locked herself out. In exasperation she rattled the door handle, but the snap lock had set itself and the door was fast. She tapped her foot angrily, staring at the door, wondering how long Mrs. Turnbull would take, knowing she didn't want to wait out in the cold dampness for her. She knew the windows were all locked, doubly protected by storm windows. Then she remembered the basement door and she leaned over the rail of the stoop trying to see if it was locked also. They had left it open for the man to start the furnace, and she hadn't gone down to lock it again. She didn't think Robert had either. She hesitated one more moment; a gust of wind blew cold rain onto the stoop, and she made up her mind. She hung the curtains on the top of the screen door and ran to the basement door and found it open. The basement was warm, but musty smelling and unaired, with a suggestion of sulphur. . . . She hurried down the steps and across to the stairs that led back up to the entrance at the kitchen door. Halfway up the steps she felt it again.

Suddenly the view before her of steps and the closed door changed, whirling out of focus, becoming different, unfamiliar, unrecognizable, and frightening. She clutched the rail, fighting terror, and horror. She closed her eyes hard, as the angles of the steps seemed to shift, becoming sharper. She thought she was going to fall, and she heard a moan. Her head was swelling, growing larger and larger, with an excruciating pain.

Then abruptly it was all gone, so suddenly that she lurched forward and would have fallen down the stairs but for the reflexive clutching of her hands for support. She half sat, half lay there for another moment, trying to get back her breath, trying to will her heart back to normal. She was breathing in gasping, choking spasms that did little to restore her. Somehow she fell and clambered up the stairs to the door. As she scrambled through the doorway, her hand landed on the greasy smear on the floor, and it burned fiercely. She ran to the sink and washed it, and she was sobbing by then. Her palm was red.

When Ellen Turnbull returned with the keys, Mandy was seated at the table drinking coffee and smoking.

"Are you all right, Mrs. Phillips? You sick?"

"I locked myself out and got back in through the basement and, like a clumsy horse, I fell coming up the stairs," Mandy said. She felt her hand tighten on the handle of her cup, but what else could she say? It had been so fast, and when it was gone, she was so normal again, what else could she say?

Mrs. Turnbull regarded her for another second, opened the door to the basement, and clicked her tongue. "You got mud on your shoes," she said. "Guess you slipped." She looked back at Mandy. "You sure you didn't hurt yourself? You look pretty pale." Mandy shook her head. "Well, I'd best wipe up that mud before someone slips again on it." She vanished, and presently she returned with a wad of paper toweling that she threw into the trash can. She stepped outside the kitchen door and came back in with the curtains. "You forgot these, I guess," she said.

"I . . . I'll hang them tomorrow," Mandy said. "I'm through for today. I'll go out as you do."

"What else could I say?" Mandy asked herself as she drove from the house. What could she say to make Robert understand? How describe something completely outside human experience? There were no words for it, everything was an approximation only. Strange, foreign, different, weird. Terror, horror, that was closer, but still it wasn't exactly right. She didn't know what words to use. She stared fixedly ahead and let her hands and feet operate the car, and the hour drive was over quickly. Inside their apartment, she paced, and in the end she knew she couldn't tell Robert what had happened to her. He would say indigestion, or nerves. The fall, the bruises, the terror, all the rest of it was part of a reaction to a momentary delusion she had suffered. And she had suffered the delusion as a result of thorough fatigue. Moving, the show, shopping, sewing, measuring. . . She was so tired that she no longer recognized her symptoms as those of fatigue, but experienced them as something else.

When Robert arrived home, she told him merely that she had slipped on mud on the basement steps, and he commiserated with her, and later massaged her aching back and legs.

The Groth knew it should wait patiently this time for the new Earthpeople to settle into the house. It seemed assured that they would stay however, and the receptive Earthman female was back. It didn't know if it had time enough to wait. It reached for her very carefully. It had forgotten how distorted the world was through their eyes, how bright the lights were, the sharp angles they used, the shining surfaces and painful colors. It longed for the gentle seas of Gron, where it could be healed, soothed by the cool waters, lulled by the gentle shapes that were dimmed with shadows and always rounded.

The Groth had learned long ago that Earthmen used light in the same manner that the Groth used shadows on Gron. There the eyes were drawn back deeply into shadows, around forms, over curves, always seeking the deepest shadow; here on Earth light was cast from objects and surfaces, repelling the eyes, making them move from one surface to another, achieving the same end: keeping the eyes in motion, forcing them to see the whole when they might settle for a part. The difference lay in the effect of the bright, shiny surfaces on the very large Groth eyes. Immediately its eyes reacted as Earthmen's eyes do after several hours on a sun-sparkling snow field. Pain, shooting lights, blindness, sometimes permanent, more often not. The Groth couldn't control the panic feeling that the surface itself was leaping at it, not merely the light being reflected dazzlingly. But worse than the physical distress, there was the instant intense hatred its touch produced. A hatred like a powerful force that drained the Groth's energy. It had touched her, but she was suddenly the invading force. It freed itself abruptly, and watched the female collapse from a safe distance.

The Groth all possessed extrasensory abilities, but only a small percentage of them had also the ability to control and order the process on a high level. Training brought about facilitation of the neuronal pathways and synapses so that, in effect, the Groth's mind was like a room with an open door, safer from intrusion than any lock could have made it. The fully trained Groth would never enter the mind of another without invitation, unless it were for a medical purpose, or other such purpose when the mind entered was in no position to give consent. When the untrained Groth probed at the mind of one trained, it found familiar images, common elementary concepts, but no formed thoughts or organized mental conversations. There was no shock. The invaded Groth merely withdrew, if the contact persisted, and it ended there. But to be so invaded by an alien intelligence was to fill each with disturbing imagery with contorted views of the world seen differently, unfamiliar dominant fears that were irrational but inescapable. If the invading power was great, as was that which the Earthmen possessed, then there was the danger of adding shock of the Groth to that of the invading mind before the contact could be broken. Herein lay the danger; herein lay insanity.

The Groth pulled back completely to rest and think. It didn't know if it would be possible to use this female after all. Others would come; it had heard them speak of others. It would probe them before it reached a decision. It would have to use one of them, or lose a priceless opportunity.

When the planet had been discovered, Earth year 1896, Gron year 14,395, the excitement on Gron had been rampant. Never had a world been found poised on the threshold of the breakthroughs that would lead to a technological civilization within the lifetimes of the Groth. Plans were made with dispatch to send observers, and computers were programmed to estimate the rate of progress of the newly found people. Dates were given in Earth terms for the advances expected: 1965, atomic energy discovery; 1980, first satellite in space; 1995, first orbiting manned spacecraft; 2010, landing on moon; 2040, landing on nearest planet; 2150, ready for contact with alien civilization. The first Gron observation station was planned, on Earth, with orbiting sky-spies, and data banks. Forty Gron years were to be allowed for this phase of the operation, with a discreet withdrawal to more distant points following that, possibly to the vicinity of the outermost planet of the system. In Earth terms, that would mean the first landing was to be made in 1920, the Groth to be picked up again in 1973. Forty Gron years, fifty-three Earth years. It was felt particularly necessary to have observers on the ground for the discovery and testing of atomic energy, when that breakthrough point arrived, but after that, when the Earthmen started to explore the nearer reaches of space, there could be no satellite of alien make in their heavens to confound them and make them suspicious and aggressive through xenophobic fears.

It was known that Earth was a dangerous planet for

Groth; it was a hot world, and the oxygen-rich atmosphere was denser than they were accustomed to, uncomfortably dense and sticky. The excessive oxygen reacted with their body chemistry in a peculiar manner, causing them to excrete in micturation and perspiration more of the sulphur of their body liquids than was healthy. Also, the spectrum of electromagnetic waves from the star of this world was less tempered by distance—Gron was two hundred million miles from its star—so that the rays, ultra-violet, infra-red, and all between were brutal on the Groth skin, and particularly hard on the very large eyes protected only by nictitating membrane, perfect in the Gron seas, and on its cool, dim land masses, but not suited for Earth's surface. Special contact lenses had been developed, and they helped, but they were a further irritant. The alkalinity of Earth's waters proved poisonous to the Groth, another mark on the debit side. But to offset some of the dangers, it was noted that the arrogance, typical of emerging people, of Earthmen in their belief that there were no other life forms served to protect the Groth in situations where their presence might be clearly indicated otherwise. So, while the mission certainly was one of hazards, it was also one in which the gains would more than offset any of the risks, and at the end of the period allotted by the computer schedule, another great world power would be welcomed to the interstellar families. But equally important, a race going through the greatest changes conceivable would be studied for the first time. A pair of lifemates was chosen, a pair well trained in the use of all equipment, with particular skills in extra-sensory development and empathy that registered in the highest range. Now only one of them still lived to carry out the mission.

Mandy wandered aimlessly about the house, one week after moving in, waiting for Robert to finish in his office, where he was closeted with his partner, Eric, and Grace, who was their secretary. The house was aglow with late afternoon sun streaming in through the windows in the front, through the double door panes, and the wide windows above the door. The cold rain had given way to very mild weather. A memory stirred of the terror she had felt on two different occasions in the house. She shrugged. She had been so tired, was still tired, but not with the urgency of the fatigue she felt the past week. She looked in at the guest room that was ready for Dwight. The left corner room was prepared for Eric, who had stayed with them for two nights already. Eric was thirty, an easy-going bachelor, willing to work in the insurance office without pushing for a bigger business, although one day, Mandy was certain, when he became sole owner of the agency, he would expand, but easily, without strain. That was all right; she just didn't want Robert taking on any more now.

Mandy was in the hall above the offices when she heard the door open, and Grace's voice saying, "Haven't you felt anything at all, Robert? I got a flash of it as soon as I came this morning. Not strong, not really bad, but something."

"You expect a house like this to be haunted," Eric said lazily, and Grace cut in:

"I never expected a house to be haunted in my life. I didn't say I think this one is haunted. I said I felt something strange. That's all."

Eric laughed and their voices drifted out of range. Mandy moved then, going to the rail to stare down at Grace's tightly waved gray hair and Eric's too long, almost flowing brown hair as they walked side by side toward the front of the house. She looked at her watch—four-thirty, cocktail time. Stiffly, she went down the stairs.

She went to the kitchen where Ellen Turnbull was finishing with the tray of ice, glasses, cheeses and crackers. "Thought you might like this," she said, "with the drinks."

"Thanks. I'll take it in," Mandy said.

"Mike will come with me in the morning," Mrs. Turnbull said. "You want him to start on the garage, or in the yard?"

"The garage, I think. If he can clear out enough space to park the cars, that'll be fine." She lifted the tray, and with her shoulder against the door, she asked, "How is the Farley boy?"

"Pete Farley's seen too many TV shows, that's all that's the matter with him. He's back in school. Wasn't nothing but a stomach ache, I told you. Told Gus that too. Damn fools, both of 'em."

As Mandy entered the living room, Eric and Grace were arguing over whether or not the fireplace would heat the room. Outside the office they argued almost constantly. They were both fighting Grace's maternal instinct, Mandy had decided.

Eric said, "Let me make a fire. It'll heat. In this climate they had to put out." He, unlike Robert, was quite at home in the country setting, flannels, sweater, wool socks. He was busy crumpling paper as he talked, and he added three logs and struck a match to it. The logs were nicely dried and caught without any trouble. Soon the fire was crackling. Robert joined them and mixed drinks for them all, then sat by Mandy on the couch. The fire was warming, and with the last rays of sunlight coming in almost horizontally now, the room was very alive and cheerful.

Eric and Robert talked quietly of the problems of moving the business. Grace looked resigned. She said to Mandy, "And there's really been no talk about this house? I can't imagine a house being empty so many years without rumors starting, noises, lights, something."

Robert's hand squeezed Mandy's briefly, and he said, "Of course, there was Pete Farley, last week. Worked here one day and got as sick as a dog. Missed two days of school. Nightmares, nervousness, sick at his stomach, but the doctor couldn't find out why. Some say it was the house did it."

Mandy couldn't control the convulsive tightening of her own hand, and Robert looked at her and winked. He was teasing Grace, thought Mandy was going along with it. It seemed incredible to her that he didn't sense her distaste for talk like this. She took a long swallow of her drink and stood up.

"The question," Grace said seriously, "is not what others think, but what the boy himself thinks. Is he willing to come back and work here again?"

"His father won't permit him to return," Mandy said coolly, starting for the door. "I have to look at the roast, be right back."

Ellen had left, and the roast was quietly spewing and spitting, and smelled of garlic. Mandy closed the oven on it. She poured herself a cup of coffee and sipped it black, wishing Tippy and Dwight would get there. She wondered if Grace were off the subject of the house and its possible ghost, and she knew that she didn't want to talk about it, or hear about it at all. Ever.

Tippy and Dwight arrived shortly after that, and there was a noisy reunion, joking, college gossip, dinner, and the inevitable tour of the house. Tippy was small, slender, almost too thin, and very lovely with black hair halfway down her back and the same long eyes that Mandy had, more heavily made up, predominant in her face, which wore no other make-up. She wore a white tunic over black tights, and would have made a beautiful magazine cover girl that night. She smoked too much and had a restless energy that could become nerve wracking. She had the intuitive understanding of mathematics in practice and abstract theory that made her very impatient with anyone who couldn't understand immediately.

Dwight was twenty-four, already the author of a textbook on Spanish literature, with a doctorate in

Romance literature. He worked for a publishing firm as a textbook editor. Mandy had never said it, not even to Robert, but she thought Dwight was a terrible bore. Tippy and Dwight had been engaged for three months.

Twice Mandy headed Grace off the subject of haunted houses, and as soon as Tippy took Dwight and Eric away to see the rest of the house, Mandy said, "Grace, I wish you wouldn't talk like that. Tippy is too young and imaginative. . . ."

"Tippy!" Grace looked at her incredulously. "That kid's not afraid of the devil himself."

"She's happy with the house. I wouldn't want you to start any doubts in her mind. . . ."

Grace looked dubious, then shrugged. "If she feels it, she'll start her own doubts. I did."

"You felt something?"

"Didn't Robert tell you?" Grace moved closer to Mandy and lowered her voice. "I'm sorry, Mandy. I was certain that Robert had told you all about it. I wouldn't have brought it up otherwise. I had a strange experience this morning. A feeling of panic, with things looking all wrong."

There was a sudden shrill scream from upstairs and both women jerked. Mandy moved before Grace did, was out the door and running up the broad stairs, and only dimly was aware of Tippy's voice, and behind her, of Grace's voice calling Robert, who had gone into his office.

"Tippy? Where are you?" The door from the third floor opened and Tippy and Dwight came down, followed by Eric. Tippy met Mandy at the head of the stairs and threw herself into Mandy's arms. "Mother! Something . . . touched me, inside! Something . . . hot. . . ." She was gasping and shivering, and Mandy's arms tightened around her, and she stared over her head at Dwight.

"What happened?"

"I don't know. We were looking at the unfinished

part, and it was dark. Eric had matches, but we still couldn't see much. Tippy was near me, she started to moan, and when I touched her, she screamed."

Robert was there then, and vaguely Mandy thought that he shouldn't have come up the stairs so fast. He was too pale. Tippy was getting her breath back, and a little color had returned to her face. Mandy thought she must be rather white also.

"Good Lord," Tippy said suddenly, clearly and in awe, "we have a ghost!"

"We are not haunted," Robert said stiffly, fifteen minutes later. They were in the living room, Mandy and Dwight on the couch with Tippy, Eric poking at the fire now burning very low with sputtering sounds, Grace and Robert in the two gold chairs. Tippy was too restless to remain quiet. She started to pace, smoking fast, frowning.

"I don't know about you, Dad," she said, "but I sort of feel that I am, or was, haunted. I never felt anything like that before."

"See how contagious talk like that can be?" Robert said bitterly to Grace.

"That isn't fair," Mandy said. "She didn't tell Tippy anything. No one did."

Eric was still poking the charred logs. He turned and said easily, "Unless it was something on the third floor."

"For God's sake. . ." Robert said, but Eric continued: "Come off it, Robert. Something happened." He looked at Tippy, who had stopped pacing to stare at him intently.

Robert swirled the gin in his glass, watching it. He was very angry, Mandy knew. He detested mysteries, didn't believe in them actually. Nerves or indigestion, that was his answer for anything out of the ordinary. A pill, or a check-up, or a simple act of willful amnesia, that was the solution, the only solution he would abide. Things without names, she thought, that's what he refused to admit, and those were the things that frightened. So he labeled events out of the norm and, with the label, could dismiss them.

Dwight said, "Eric, let's stop all this now. It was strange and quiet and hot up there. I felt it too, but stale air and stillness, nothing more than that." Mandy almost nodded. How like Robert he was.

"Something else," Tippy said firmly. "Eric's right. We have to look at it logically and try to understand what it was." She grinned at Robert who was glaring at her and Eric. "Relax, Dad. My game, but you don't have to play if you don't want to." She turned to Grace then. "Let's compare notes. What was it that you didn't tell me? You felt something here too?"

Grace looked from her to Mandy, who shrugged. Grace then said, "I'm not sure. Something made me feel complete panic, my head hurt, and everything seemed to go weird all at once." She took a long drink, emptying her glass.

Tippy nodded. "That's two of us. I didn't know about that. I couldn't have dittoed what I didn't know. That's how it was with me. I felt something, like a hot wire in my head. Hot and moving. The match light got all twisted and just wrong, and I had to close my eyes. I couldn't stand the way things looked." She looked at Robert. "Dad, it doesn't do any good to say it didn't happen. It did. Twice."

"Three, or possibly four times," Mandy said tiredly. She told of her two experiences, and Robert stared at her disbelievingly. "I think you might have felt it, too, darling," she said. "Last weekend, while you slept. You groaned as if with pain, or fear. Then it was over and you returned to normal sleep."

"Good Christ!" Robert said suddenly. "You three women! Talk about nerves and mass hysteria! Look at what you're doing to yourselves! Just because some stupid neighborhood kid got sick and his father is a fool! Mandy, you know that's what started all this, don't you? That boy got sick. Probably he smoked a couple of cigarettes and got sick from them. So you let it build up to something big and mysterious in your mind, and now Tippy is feeling it, and Grace."

Mandy stared at him, wanting to believe him, willing herself to believe him. She remembered the way the stairs had gone too sharp, angled, and unfamiliar, and she looked down at her hands in her lap.

Grace stood up then. "I have to be on my way," she said. She looked at Tippy, and then to Mandy. "Are you both all right? Are you sta—?" She didn't finish the question, but said more briskly, "I have to be going."

Robert saw her to her car, and while they were gone, Eric said, "Tippy, no one is in my apartment this weekend. Why don't you—?"

"Will you knock it off!" Dwight said angrily.

"Oh, Dwight, shut up," Tippy said. She looked at Eric and grinned. "Why don't you go back if you think something is here?"

"Because I'm curious about it, I guess. You see, I don't believe in ghosts either."

"Well, that sums up my feeling exactly. No one believes in ghosts, and yet, there is something that we can't see, something horrible, completely terrible and loathsome. We are all so sane, so quietly, dependably, self-assuredly sane," she said, almost mockingly. "But something here isn't sane at all." She shivered and hugged herself, moving closer to the fire.

Robert returned and looked at them suspiciously. He poured another drink. Mandy started to protest that he was drinking more than he should, but she didn't say the words. They all needed an extra drink, or two.

They talked awhile; then they broke up the group, and Mandy and Robert went to their room. Robert was still angry with her, she knew, and they said little as they prepared for bed. She heard Eric putting another log on the fire, but gradually the house became very quiet. She lay staring at the ceiling, knowing when Robert finally fell asleep, after lying too stiff and too silent at her side for a long time. She thought of the past when such anger at bedtime would have had her in tears, and the making up would have had her in wilder tears. She smiled. Her hand touched his back gently. She dozed and woke with a start. She hadn't meant to fall asleep at all. There was something that she had to try.

It was nearly three-thirty when she slipped from the bed quietly. She got on her robe and slippers and left the bedroom without making a sound. Eric had left the hall lights on as she had asked him, and the shadows filled the balcony with strange shapes. The other bedroom doors were closed, and the house was still. She went down the stairs, and when she got to the bottom, she began to call to it, soundlessly, concentrating on the words she was thinking at it:

You! Whatever you are, leave her alone! Don't you touch her again! I'm not afraid of you now, I can face you now, but leave her alone! You understand what I'm saying! Leave her alone. Come out now that I'm ready for you. You caught me in surprise before, but I'm ready for you. . . .

She knew she could drive it away. She felt the same exultant thrill that she used to feel before a modeling show, that she still felt before her fashions were shown, the same challenge, the same awareness of her ability to meet the challenge. She waited, but the house continued silent and empty. She called to it again and still felt nothing. She walked into the living room where embers from the fire glowed. She would wait half an hour for it. She put a log on the embers and blew on them until a tiny flame licked the log and started to grow. She sat on the floor before the small fire and waited for it to answer her challenge.

And when it did, she was not prepared for it. She was watching the leaping fire and suddenly it was there again, something groping inside her head, making it swell, making it hurt. The fire froze and the colors went wrong, became fearful and blindingly bright,

bringing tears to her eyes. She blinked hard and started
to rise, but the room was tilting at terrifying angles,
and the walls and floor were threatening. She felt that
her head was going to burst with the presence, and the
pain and terror grew and became unbearable. She felt
nausea rise and ebb and rise again, and suddenly she
was violently sick and still the presence grew and con-
sumed her. It was vile and repulsive, and she screamed
and fell to the floor with her eyes closed, unable now
to open them at all, horrified at the appearance of the
room, at the threatening walls and floor and the
hideous colors and the foul air. She was sick again,
heaving and retching, and sobbing, and she had to get
back to the vlen where it was safe. She began inching
along the floor, with her eyes closed tightly, sucking
in the foul air that was achingly hot now. She had to
rid herself of the heavy clothing that was smothering
her, and not opening her eyes she began to claw at
the thick, rough material. She shrank from the contact,
but with it on, she couldn't breathe. The bad air was
weakening her. She bumped into something and had
to open her eyes to see her way from the oppressive
room. One of *them* entered, and there was much noise,
and suddenly blinding lights were stabbing her. She
shrieked and rolled to protect her eyes, and one of
them touched her. She lashed out at it. Unendurable
pain exploded in her head and everything stopped.

The Groth had been dozing in the tank bed when it
felt the pulling of the female's mind. It was as strong
as a death call of a lifemate, as strong as the fear call
of a young one in the seas, as strong as the birthing
call of a female lifemate. It had elements of each of
them, and was as irresistible. The Groth found itself
dragging its painful body from the vlen, into the
bad air of the lowest level of the building, its mind
engaged and almost helpless under the barrage of fear
and repulsion of the female Earthman. It fell to the
floor writhing and hissing in agony, and did not know

that the female was also writhing above it. It secreted dangerously and became weaker, less able to ward off the death wishes of the female. Abruptly the contact was broken. The Groth was unable to move afterward, however, and lay for hours waiting for strength to return.

It thought about the decision to position the vlen so near an inhabited building, and it realized that the decision had been wrong. They should have remained in the spaceship. But they had reasoned that there was a remote danger of being followed to it; also being so near the Earthpeople had been as fruitful as they thought it would be. The Groth's thoughts ranged back over the years, over all the things that had gone wrong.

The Groth had built a tunnel when they first arrived at the house and decided to use it to protect the vlen, hidden deep under the unexcavated area. The tunnel led to the woods half a mile away, emerging aboveground in a dense thicket, the opening well hidden by boulders. After the death of the child years ago when the Groth had decided to leave the vlen and live in the ship, it had waited for a dark night, then had left in the one-man craft that was kept in the tunnel. It planned to bring the ship to the woods and park it there, obliterate all traces of the vlen, then fly to the vast uninhabited lands to the north. It flew, skimming the treetops, to the site of the spacecraft that the two Groth had hidden in a valley in the woods. They had partially buried the spacecraft, covering the mound it made with earth and stones and boulders, planting shrubs over all, so that in the end, it was impossible to see anything out of the ordinary there. By removing one of the bushes, access to the craft was simple, requiring no loss of time. The Groth flew directly to the site and stared in disbelief. Water covered the valley. It flew to the end of the valley and found a concrete dam, flew low enough over it to make out the inscription on a plaque: Falsmouth Reservoir, N. Y. C.

The Groth located the craft under forty feet of water, then returned to the vlen. It could get to it, but the water made it more awkward, made sealed clothing necessary, as well as the construction of an air lock. It worked on the arrangements, and on the next dark rainy day, knowing that Earthmen seldom ventured out in such weather, it returned to the reservoir. It almost plunged into the lake before it realized that Earthmen were there, hugging the shore line behind crude shelters. It searched its memories for a reason, and recalled that Earthmen hunted birds during this season. Again it returned to the vlen. The next visit was after the lake had frozen over, and again the Groth was frustrated. Earthmen dotted the smooth gray surface, fishing through the ice.

In the seasons that followed, the lake became more and more inaccessible to the Groth. It had become a favored resort area. In the summer swimmers and boaters crowded the shores and the surface of the water; in the fall the hunters arrived, then the ice fishermen and ice skaters; a ski run skirted it; chalets were built, and cabins, and a hotel. . . .

They were bad years for the Groth, still suffering the loss of its lifemate, and the remorse of having caused, albeit indirectly, the deaths of several of the Earthmen. The latent extrasensory abilities of the Earthmen had not been foreseen, thus not allowed for in the planning. If the Groth now moved the spacecraft, there would be more damage done to the emerging people, possibly more deaths. If only the lifemate were still alive; the two of them could ward off the untrained probings of the Earthmen through reinforcement of one another, but alone? The Groth knew that alone it might slip and allow one or more of the probes to pass through. It was not the skill of the Groth that was lacking, although thorough shielding required fierce concentration; it was the lack of training and control of the Earthmen. The use of a great latent power was as dangerous to the user as it was to the one against whom it was used, and if there were several Earthmen probing randomly, the Groth feared that it would not be able to withstand their combined force, nor would they escape unscathed. Many of them would die, others go mad. It could not move until the last possible moment had arrived, and perhaps by then, it would be in contact with the Groth ship due to pick it up, and a new plan would be forthcoming.

So the Groth settled back into the vlen under the house, and monitored its equipment. From time to time Earthmen had come to the house, and often building had been started, but always they had left again. In 1957, Earth year, the Groth made another attempt to leave Earth and wait in a distant orbit for the ship from Gron. The Earthmen who called themselves Russians had orbited a satellite, years ahead of schedule.

The Groth retrieved the air lock bubble it had constructed years before, and donned the two-fabric suit that would allow it to work under water, waterproof on the outside, sulphuric-acid proof inside, and it went once more to the lake, choosing the hours before daylight as the least likely of all to be interrupted. It slid into the water unobserved, and went directly to the spacecraft, now covered with several feet of silt. The Groth tested the waters, only to find them even more strongly alkaline than it had believed, and it knew it would have to work fast. There were bits of jagged containers in the area, both glass and metal, and it removed them carefully: the suit would rip with ease. The Groth swam around the ship then, inspecting it, and suddenly felt a tug on its suit and investigated to find that a small barbed piece of metal was stuck on its leg. It didn't attempt to remove it, still fearing a tear, but broke the line that was attached to it, and continued to inspect the area around the ship. It located the door and started to remove the silt there.

On the shore, a man nodding over the fishing line jerked awake when there was a tug on the spin rod lying across his knees. He reeled in the broken line and studied it intently. A grin split his face, and whistling softly, he tied a new hook to the line, added a heavier weight and a small minnow, and cast it to the exact spot where he had got the strong strike.

The Groth worked hard and finally uncovered the metal of the ship. It was pitted with corrosion, but the Groth knew that was the outer layer only and was not concerned. It didn't see the weighted line sinking through the water behind it, coming to rest on the bottom, with the minnow swimming vigorously in circles that were within inches of the Groth's legs. The minnow twisted back on itself and got loose from the hook, darting away. The hook came to rest then, and the nylon line blended with the water so that no part of the rig was visible, except the dull hook two feet above the floor of the lake. The Groth turned to get the air lock, and as it brushed by the hook, it was snagged. There was an immediate reaction from the man on the shore, who jerked the line hard, ripping a straight tear eight inches long on the leg of the suit. The Groth felt the sting of the alkaline waters and writhed from the touch. The reaction of the water with its acidic perspiration caused steam and clouds around it, obscuring the line even more, and the Groth fumbled about with both hands searching for the thing that had caught it. The man tried to reel in, and again the fabric tore, but this time the Groth found the line and broke it, and it was yanked away with the sudden release of tension. The Groth was weakening quickly, and it swam back to the small craft that was also full of water now. It closed the door and started the pump, and even before the craft was dry, it started to move through the water. The Groth located the Earthman on the shore and searched the area, but no one else was there. The Earthman might be curious about what was down there. . . . He might dive down and find the bared metal of the spacecraft before the silt again crept over it. The

Groth didn't want to think about the Earthman and his possible actions, didn't want to have to injure him, didn't want to have to touch his mind at all. It was getting out of the soaked suit as fast as it could, but it continued to watch the Earthman, who was standing on the shore now, staring at the water over the spacecraft. Bubbles, the Groth thought. There were bubbles. The Earthman waded out into the water, and the Groth reached out and touched his mind. The man staggered and fell in the knee-deep water. The Groth made him move back to the shore, rolling him gently, then left him. The Earthman was dead.

The Groth was weakening too fast then to pay any further attention to the Earthman, to the lake, or other possible observers. It left the water, flying almost straight up, turned to the woods, and flew back to the tunnel and the vlen and the life-giving bed tank. It lay there resting for days, hovering between dreams and reality, finding itself in the dream life on the seas of Gron, then again in the tank bed, then again in the corrosive waters of the reservoir lake killing the Earthman, over and over.

The Groth had made its report, had sent the message aloft to the data bank in orbit, and it knew that its action would be exonerated. One of the worst things a civilization could do to another was to divert it from its own development through the premature disclosure of techniques far in advance of its own, and the discovery of the Groth spaceship would do that, so the death had been necessary. Still the Groth suffered. It decided not to try again to leave Earth unless that was the only way to avoid being discovered.

Its recovery was slow and less than complete, and it knew that until it returned to Gron and received the care of healers, it would continue to bear the effects of its exposure to the lime water of the lake, and the inhalation of the gases that had formed from the reaction of the acid and alkaline.

Events were moving very fast on Earth, and the

Groth was forced to redesign its spy mechanisms several times. Finally it fashioned bee-like, remote-controlled units that it could send to any point undetected. The unit landed on a tree when it reached its destination, bored into the trunk, and reported to the Groth all that went on within its range. This proved satisfactory, and the Groth's trips beyond the vlen became less frequent. Each trip now was a major risk; Earthmen had developed uncanny methods of detection, and there were constant sky watchers on duty everywhere. The Groth was content not to have to risk exposure, and each year the thought of venturing outside became less desirable. Periodically, however, it did fly over the lake and check on the position of the spaceship under the water, and twice it went into the lake and inspected the hull of the ship. The corrosion was increasing, but still not dangerously. The silt was much deeper, and with each year the possibility of discovery of the ship became more remote. The Groth was satisfied with the arrangement.

Then, almost ten Earth years after its accident in the lake, the Groth was again shocked into action. The data-bank satellite was being scanned. It sent the message to the vlen, and the computer there interpreted the scanning as a search operation being carried out, with the probability high that all foreign objects were being sought out and marked for destruction as hazards to the fast growing space developments of the Earthmen.

Again the Groth had to go to the lake and enter the poisonous waters to gain access to the ship, where it had equipment to change the orbit of the satellite. It worked quickly in the dark, but as it worked it became aware of the images pressing against its brain: fear, hatred, dread, disgust. . . . It had been seen this time. A score of men were on the shore, most of them armed, all of them certain something had entered the lake. The Groth withdrew without entering the minds of any of the men; it was enough that they were there,

and that they were broadcasting to it. There was no
need to probe further. It hastened its own work; its
first duty was to alter the orbit of the satellite. It
worked on the new course, deciding on an orbit far
beyond the moon, and within an hour it was reassured
that the satellite had moved out and away from the
questing devices that had found it. Then it turned its
attention to the activity on the shore. The men had
been joined by others, and the entire south shore of
the lake was buzzing with excitement. If necessary, the
Groth would leave the area in the spaceship, but not
yet. The vlen had to be dismantled also. It would
wait and take action that seemed appropriate when
the men moved.

Daylight came, and the men sent divers into the lake.
Three of them fanned out in the direction of the ship,
and the foremost of them carried a metal detection
mechanism that was crude, but effective. The Groth
neutralized it; the ship had been on power since its
arrival in the area, so that no metal detection device
yet known to man could have found it. What the
Groth feared was their visual ability to spot the metal
in the water where the silt had been removed for entry.
The Groth continued to watch the progress of the
Earthmen.

In the afternoon the divers departed, and a few
surface swimmers appeared on the scene. The Groth
ignored them. The next day, there were only three of
the men on the alert, and at night they were relieved
by two others, who were also wary. The Groth probed
very gently; these two were of a different nature. It
didn't want to enter either of them, so it simply
watched them from a distance throughout the night.
It learned that they were private investigators who
made a practice of running to earth flying saucer re-
ports. The Groth permitted itself to relax once more.
No Earthpeople paid very much attention to them
and their kind. The danger was much less than it had
assumed at first. The following night it would leave

the area. Its spy system would alert it to any danger
to the ship, and it could return if it appeared necessary.

The next night the Groth exchanged water for air
in the lock very slowly, so that the bubbles released
would be minute, unnoticeable. Outside the ship, it
waited for the silt to recover the ship, and it inspected
the hull carefully to make certain that it was not
visible. Above the quiet water, a faint odor of sulphur
floated softly, crossing the lake, rousing one of the
men who refused to admit that nothing had entered
the lake. He jerked wide awake. The same smell he
had noticed the other time!

He jabbed his elbow into the ribs of his companion,
and together they left their sleeping bags, and crawled
to the edge of the woods and watched. The first man
pulled a walkie-talkie from his pocket and whispered
into it excitedly until he received an answer. He hefted
his rifle and waited. When the snub-nosed capsule slid
from the water, spotlights flared, and there were
sounds of rifle fire.

The Groth almost fainted from the excruciating pain
of the explosion of light that blinded it. Planning to
work at night, to fly only at night, it had not provided
itself with the dark contact lenses, and it could not
protect its eyes against the glare. It groped for the
control to opaque the windows of the small craft,
and it accelerated blindly, hearing rifle fire at the
same moment; it felt the impact as projectiles struck
the craft. It flew straight into the woods, hoping it
was high enough, not able to see at all now. It
careened off the topmost branch of an ancient pine
tree, and the craft reeled, but didn't go out of control.
The Groth climbed again. There was more rifle fire,
and this time one of the projectiles did damage the
craft, but it was still climbing, and no more of the
shots reached it. The Groth leveled out after another
moment, and still flying blindly, waited for its eyes to
recover.

Several minutes later the Groth was turned and heading back toward the vlen. It could see again, blurrily, but enough. Pressure in the craft was dropping. There was a tendency to list to the left. Daylight was coming quickly now, and it knew it had to seek cover within the next few minutes or risk being seen in daylight. Also, the leak in the craft was admitting the heavy oxygenized air mixture that brought about dizziness. The Groth didn't dare put the craft on automatic in order to search for and mend the leak; the craft might be heavily damaged and the automatic controls out of coordination with the vlen. Even as the Groth thought this, the craft lurched and dropped in altitude. The Groth fought to right the craft, tilting dangerously to the left, and finally knew it had to land short of the safety of the tunnel. The craft was going to crash if it wasn't taken down now. There was sluggish response to the controls, and again the lurching drop. The Groth landed precariously in a small clearing and sat for several moments until his whirling thoughts focused once more on the problem at hand. Hide the craft in the tunnel. Get out of the thick atmosphere, back to the good air in the vlen. Two objectives. The sun came out dazzlingly. The objectives might be insurmountable.

For two hours the Groth struggled with the disabled craft, guiding it on low power around trees, over rocks, up and down ravines. The Groth wore a hood over its head, made by tearing up the protective garment and carefully peeling away one layer of material. The hood helped protect its eyes, but there was no protection against the rich air, and the heat of the sun. The air was damaging its lungs, perhaps beyond repair this time. The effects of the old accident added to its discomfort. Breathing was a torture, and the loss of body fluids was alarmingly high. The heat of the sun, poorly screened through the trees' branches, was devastating, and it excreted more and more fluids to protect its outer skin layers. The craft got away from it suddenly and skittered over the ground, bearing to the left constantly, and vanished over a cliff. The Groth staggered after it, not seeing the edge of the cliff until it could no longer stop, and it too tumbled over and down, and when it regained consciousness, some minutes later, it knew that it had broken inside.

Delirious, only half aware of what it was doing, the Groth continued to grope for the tunnel and its safety. The next time it was fully aware of its actions, it was within the tunnel, gasping and choking on the good air it was sucking in. It left the craft behind the first screen in the tunnel and staggered to the tank bed and collapsed into it. The tank bed sealed, bathed the Groth, cooled down to the lowest permissible temperature, and started to cure the many superficial cuts and scrapes and bruises of the Groth. The interior wounds could not be healed by the tank bed; they required a doctor's probing thoughts and fingers.

The Groth knew now that it could not reach its ship at rest under the lake. The small one-man craft that made possible its visits to the lake had been damaged too badly to be repaired, first by the rifle fire, then even more by the fall over the cliff. It could only destroy the ship from the vlen, and with it destroy much of the lake and many of the Earthpeople in the vicinity. Then it would have to set the automatic destruct controls of the satellite, and finally eradicate all traces of the vlen and itself along with it. Or train an Earthperson so that there was real communication, so that the Earthperson could be sent into the lake and bring the ship out and back to the woods near the vlen. The Groth then could depart in it and leave no traces of its visit on Earth behind to befuddle the Earthmen. But first it had to train one of the wild Earth minds to communicate. It would take the same kind of orderedness that the lifemate had developed, thinking not in primal images, but in controlled symbols so that the Groth could see through the Earthman's eyes, think with his brain. It had thought the female would do, but at its touch, the female's rational brain was instantly submerged by her hatred and fear. It probed the others and found the same reaction. It brooded over the latent power they had, and their inability to use it. The female's latest assault, almost successful, proved to the Groth that they were still savages, all of them, who would kill without thought any other being they encountered. Its thoughts became more and more despairing as it rested and waited for strength enough to return to the vlen.

Mandy opened her eyes and stared about her in bewilderment. Eric's room, his apartment. She had found it for him. She tried to recall the night before, her childish challenge to the . . . thing: a blank. Silently she got out of the bed and crossed the room to the only door, which was slightly open. She looked through to the living room beyond, and then she breathed in relief.

Robert was asleep in a deep chair, and beyond him there was Tippy with her dark head close to Eric as they conversed in tones too low to catch. Mandy pushed the door open more, and Tippy's face lifted and she ran across the room when she saw her mother standing there.

"Are you all right? How do you feel?"

"I'm fine. Weak, and starved, but all right." Mandy stared at her daughter and asked slowly, "What happened?"

Eric had joined them, and now Robert stirred and came wide awake in a second, with a look of fear and anxiety on his face such as she never had seen there.

"Will someone tell me what happened?" she said again. Robert caught her in his arms and held her close to him so hard that it hurt. That bad, she wondered. What could have been that bad? She pushed back gently and stared at his gray face. "I'm all right, darling. Really, all right. Relax now, okay?"

Robert didn't release her, but his arms loosened a

little, and she twisted to look at Eric. He said, "We found you in a faint on the floor of the living room, near the hallway door. We couldn't wake you up, so we brought you here."

She knew that wasn't all of it, but she accepted it for the time being. She didn't know if she wanted to hear any more of it than that, not right now anyway.

"Where's Dwight?" Mandy asked.

"He wanted to go back for some clothes," Tippy said. "He'll tell Mrs. Turnbull that we won't need her today." She grinned briefly and added, "The story is that I had an attack of appendicitis, and we'll be tied up at the hospital for the day."

Eric brought coffee then and they all sipped it silently. It had to have been dreadful, Mandy thought. They were all terrified, and Robert and Tippy couldn't keep their eyes off her. What had she done?

Eric stood up. "I'll go help Dwight," he said.

"I'll come with you," Tippy said quickly.

"NO! Not you!" Mandy heard the strident tone of her voice. Her hand clamped on Tippy's wrist hard and the girl sat down again, the color drained from her face suddenly. "You mustn't go back, ever," Mandy said, forcing a normalcy she didn't feel.

"Then you do know . . ."

"I don't remember what happened last night, but I know that you can't go there. Promise me."

"I'll stay with you here until they get back," Tippy said. She looked up at Eric. "Call us when you get there, will you?"

"I'm coming with you," Robert said heavily. Mandy half rose and he pushed her back down gently. "It'll be all right, honey. I'll pack enough for a few days, and we can get rested and then decide what we want to do. Meanwhile, no one is going to stay there overnight again, and we won't go there alone."

Dwight saw Mrs. Turnbull standing outside the garage talking to a leggy boy whose red hair claimed him as her son. He hesitated, then went inside the house. Probably she didn't realize that no one was there, he thought. She probably thought they were all sleeping late. He glanced toward the living room, saw again the writhing figure on the floor, hissing and shrieking, and he shuddered. He had seen people acting like that in his abnormal psych lab, and he knew that sooner or later Tippy and her father would have to face up to it. Poor Tippy. He got his things quickly, then went back down the stairs. Mrs. Turnbull would have to get Mandy's clothes.

At the kitchen he called her, but there was no answer. Then he heard the boy's voice yelling. He ran outside and saw the boy racing across the yard. The tall red-headed woman met him at the door to the garage and shook him hard. The boy was pointing toward the house and talking. Dwight left the stoop and approached the door standing open, leading down to the basement. The boy and his mother came up to him. She said, "He says there's some kind of a big animal down there, dead, or hurt. He says it ain't nothing he ever seen before. You'd best not go down alone, mister."

"There's no one else here," Dwight said, pausing at the top step. He couldn't see anything in the gloom of the far end of the basement. "Where is it?" he asked the boy.

"Way back, by the dirt cellar back there. It's breathing hard, like it's dying." He breathed hard himself. "I don't know what it is."

Dwight shrugged and started down.

"Where's the Phillips?" Mrs. Turnbull called.

"Tippy got sick, and they had to take her to a doctor," he said, remembering the story they would give out. He stopped to let his eyes adjust to the darker, shadowed area. "Where are the lights?" he called up.

"I'll get them on," Mrs. Turnbull said. "They're at the head of the steps."

Dwight walked a few feet into the gloom, and it wasn't as dark as he had thought at first. He saw nothing, but there was a curious odor in the air. Not like the zoo, but musky, like an animal in the wilds, where the body odor was mixed with pine scent, and earth smells, and sulphur. He sniffed and took several more steps. There were deeper shadows along the wall, around the furnace, and there was a lot of junk piled there. He saw the door that must lead to the dirt cellar and wished Mrs. Turnbull would hurry with the lights. The shadows were just boxes and bundles of rugs, he decided, kicking one of them. There was no sound, no heavy breathing, nothing but the odor. He took another step and at the same moment the light came on.

Something screamed, a hoarse, inhuman sound of agony, and one of the bundles writhed and streaked out, striking Dwight on the leg. His entire leg burned and he stumbled, yelling also then. He rolled, trying to get away, and his hand touched it, and he screamed again with pain and fear. It was seven or eight feet long, and gray. He could see great, round eyes then, and a mouth opening and closing, uttering the agonizing cries, and long arms sweeping toward him, clutching the air with too many, too flexible fingers. He struck at it, and the thing swept over him, mingling its screams with his, bathing him in fire. Dwight convulsed in terror and pain that was unendurable; he stiffened, then went limp.

When Eric and Robert arrived, Mrs. Turnbull had already sent her son home, and the sheriff was at the house waiting for the state troopers. They reconstructed the events as best they could, deciding that there had been an animal, that it had lunged at Dwight, and in his efforts to elude it, he had upset acid on himself. They could find no such animal, nor did they find a container for acid, but, neither did they find anything else to fit the facts. Dwight had died of heart failure, the medical examiner said at the autopsy later that week, but he had suffered acid burns over most of his body.

A group of troopers searched the house, they tore open all the boxes and bundles in the basement, they examined the walls for seams that would indicate other rooms, they poked rods into the dirt walls of the wine cellar to make certain the unexcavated portion was actually unexcavated, and they found nothing. The case came to an uneasy conclusion which satisfied nobody.

The Groth had wanted only to be left alone then, but instead of peace another of the Earthmen had come. First a child, then a male adult Earthman. And the Groth had killed the male adult Earthman. Again it mourned for another's death, and again it knew there had been nothing else for it to do; their own hatred killed them.

Quiet descended on the house after a hectic period during which many Earthmen with much noise searched for the vlen. The Groth didn't sleep during that time, didn't monitor its equipment; it did nothing but concentrate on keeping the probes away, keeping its presence concealed. The Earthmen left once more. And while the Groth recuperated, it made plans for the next arrival of Earthmen.

Mandy lay on the hot sand listening to the endless surf, trying not to think any more. She pleaded with something, herself? Please no more, let me be for a little while, let me rest for a little while. The thoughts didn't go away. She could feel the presence of Robert, but they didn't speak then. Why don't you hold me just once, she thought, and tell me it wasn't my fault. Just once. Even if you don't mean it. She didn't know what Robert thought any more. She didn't know what she thought most of the time. If only they would get a letter from Tippy. If only she would write and let them know she was all right now, that she was having a good time, or at least a busy time. Next week they would go back to Manhattan, and Laura would return for the summer, and they had to tell her something, but not the truth, not the false truths that no one told any longer. The lies and half truths and the silent lies were so much more real than the simple truths, now that they wove stories and tried to remember the details of the falsehoods, and tripped and stumbled their way through them, and never looked directly at each other any more.

She wondered if Robert had any idea that she had overheard him on the telephone with their doctor, asking advice on her behalf. She had listened and his words had filled her with ice. Because she couldn't tell him in words, couldn't make him understand that something had happened; he assumed nothing had. The walls around other people always seemed so obvious, she had believed none existed between her and Robert. But it was there, invisible, unbreachable. The thoughts whirled and her tense body didn't relax at all until she became very hot and had to return to the ocean to cool off again.

Robert watched her walking back, and she knew that there was fear behind his gaze, fear for her, for them. They had to talk about money, about plans for the house now, about Tippy. . . . They had to talk. Maybe tonight, she promised herself. Maybe they would be able to break through the silence that had enveloped them, and worse than the silence, the meaningless chatter that they engaged in while dining or doing any of the things where silence would draw attention to them.

Tippy walked back and forth before Eric's apartment for almost an hour before he appeared. When he saw her, his face set in hard lines and his hand on her arm was rough. "Where the hell have you been? Don't you know your mother is almost crazy worrying about you?"

"But I told her. . . ." Tippy pulled away and looked about the people passing them, and she said, "Let's go inside. I have to talk to someone."

Eric made her a drink and she sipped it, not knowing now where to start, what to say. She was grateful when Eric broke the silence.

"First, have you been in touch with Mandy recently? She got a letter returned after you left your apartment in London. No forwarding address."

Tippy said, "Damn, I asked my friend to save any mail until I told her where to send it. I didn't know that." She looked at the phone, but didn't go near it yet. "I'll call them in a few minutes," she said.

"Have you been all right? You look like hell."

Tippy touched her face wonderingly. She hadn't noticed particularly. She shrugged. "I'm all right, I guess. I got through the finals okay, so I must be all right." Suddenly she jumped up and went to the window and stood looking out, with her back to Eric. "What happened back there? What was it?"

"I don't know," he said. He finished his drink.

"Dad thinks Mother communicated her own nervous breakdown to the rest of us somehow, made us experience it with her. Somehow." Tippy's voice held disbelief.

"That was easier for him to accept than the thought of a ghost," Eric said. "Pathological telepathy has been written about in the journals, and even if you don't want to believe in it, it's easier to buy than the return of the dead."

Still not looking at him, Tippy said in a very low voice, "But what if he's wrong?" She turned then and her voice was vehement when she continued. "Something killed Dwight. It wasn't a projected nervous breakdown! It wasn't! He was as unaffected by Mother's attack as if it hadn't happened at all. He was beyond touch as far as her supposed telepathy is concerned."

Eric poured himself another drink, a small one, more

to be doing something than because he wanted it. He said, "I didn't tell you before, Tippy. I'm sorry about Dwight. It was a tough thing for you. . . ."

She shrugged. "I don't know what would have happened with us. I think, when I can think about it, that eventually we would have broken apart, but I'll never know." She looked at her glass and drank from it slowly.

They were both silent for several moments. Then Eric said, "What are you going to do now?"

"I don't know. I feel like I have to find out what happened at that house, and I don't know how, or where to start. If Dad is right, it should be perfectly safe to go back, but if he's wrong . . . then something murdered Dwight, and that something is driving my mother crazy. Either way, I have to find out."

Eric said emphatically, "You can't go back there."

Tippy looked at him strangely. "Why? What do you know? Has something else happened?"

He hesitated only a moment, then he pulled papers from a drawer and began spreading them out. "I've done some investigating," he said. "The house was perfectly all right until about 1920, give or take a year or two. In newspapers at that time there were stories about strange lights, and the owners of the house wrote that they had acquired a ghost." Tippy shook her head, rejecting the ghost, and he said, "If you have only two theories presented, and you can accept neither of them, what next? You have to strike out to find a new theory. No nervous breakdown, no ghost, then what? Postulate an alien creature, and you can fit the rest of the facts into an intelligible pattern. Nothing else does."

Tippy stared at him with narrowed eyes, as if suspecting that he was joking with her. Her gaze became more concentrated, and finally she nodded. "Okay, go on. I don't know if I can believe that or not, but I like it better than a haunt."

"Right. So everything settled down again, and the

house remained peaceful for twelve years. The family, a Dutch importer and seven kids, servants, relatives, were very happy in the house. Then in 1932 something happened to shake all that. According to the accounts I could find, the wife died of a heart attack and two of the kids became raving maniacs overnight practically. Six months later he moved the rest of them, simply walked out of the house one day and never came back. People were sent to pack the furniture and take up carpets, and all the rest. A year later, the property was sold to John Prentiss, his wife, and her three children by a previous marriage. They stayed only two months. One of the children, a seven-year-old boy, died of what was diagnosed as acute respiratory infection at that time. The wife ran away with the two other children, and John Prentiss stayed on in the house for another two weeks. When someone came to see him, he was almost starved, practically catatonic—with grief, it was said at the time. He has since recovered, but has no memory whatever of those last weeks in the house. I talked to him."

Tippy was staring at him in fascination by then, and when he stopped, she sat down abruptly. "So there is something that lives in that house!"

"We don't know that," Eric said.

"And the other owners? What about them?"

"None of them ever lived in the house after that. Each time it changed hands, the new owners either planned changes, or started changes—like the new heating system—and then decided against living there. I talked to only one of them, Mrs. Herschel Myers. She is beautiful, you wouldn't believe unless you could see her. Weighs at least three hundred pounds, tall, strong, fiery black eyes. She and her husband escaped from Poland, walking clear across Europe to the Channel and crossed over on a raft made of saplings tied together with strips of clothing. Unbelievable. But they got to England, and after the war, they came here. In 1947 they bought the house and went to camp out in it for a weekend, and she says that she had a fight with the devil that weekend, and that while he didn't win, she knew that the house was his, and she didn't care to share it with him." He grinned and spread his hands apart. "They kept ownership of the house until 1959 when cancer killed the husband. She needed the money, or she never would have sold it. The Plainview Development Corporation bought it for an investment property, and they got stuck with it. So when your father came along, to handle insurance for the president of the corporation, he mentioned the house and its price, ridiculously low, as you know, and it changed hands again."

"If it lives there, we can find it," Tippy said softly. "We know what we're looking for—something long and gray. That's what Mike Turnbull said about what he saw."

"The official report says it was probably an injured dog down there, that it ran away after leaping at Dwight and spilling acid all over him, and that it took the container away with it."

Tippy didn't even bother to answer that. "We can draw it out, signal to it and make it reveal itself. . . ."

"How?"

"Mathematical symbols. There are constants that apply, no matter what system it uses. The speed of light, simple counting, *pi*, multiplication tables. . . . That's no problem. But how to get it to understand that we mean no harm."

"Do we understand that?" Eric asked. "Remember it killed Dwight, and it had Mandy on the floor. . . ."

Tippy paled slightly, but her face lost none of its intent look. "They were both unprepared for it, but we know what we're doing. That makes the difference."

Eric stood up and stretched. "Let's go out and have some dinner and discuss this. We have to be absolutely certain of what we're up to, what we'll do if it does come out of hiding, what system we'll use, how we'll recognize its answer." He took her arm and pulled her from the couch where she was still sitting, staring in concentration straight ahead. "Come on. I think that's it, but let's go over it all first. Dinner."

It was a very warm afternoon when Eric and Tippy drove from the city to the house in the country. Eric had got off at noon, and they had done some shopping, so that it was almost three when they arrived. The house looked uncared for already, the grass slightly unkempt, some leaves plastered against the screening of the porch, the drapes closed on all the windows.

Tippy shivered. "Want to change your mind?" Eric asked. She shook her head.

"Let's go inside and have a sandwich," Tippy said. They took the bags from the car, and while Eric opened windows, Tippy made ham and cheese sandwiches. They drank beer and ate without talking. Afterward Tippy said, "Where do you think we should try first?"

"Basement, I guess. Seems the most likely spot."

She nodded. They carried the apparatus down the stairs and set up the buzzer and the recorder that Eric had bought. Tippy looked about hesitantly. The basement was dimly lighted and cool after the heat of the upstairs, and there was a noticeable lack of fresh air, but otherwise it seemed perfectly normal. They had the recorder and the buzzer on a workbench that Eric had dragged to the center of the floor. The bundles of rags and rugs had been removed, so that nothing but the bench was in sight. She started to count with the buzzer: one—one, two—one, two, three—one, two, three, four—one, two, three, four, five . . . then again and again. After the third time, they waited, Eric's finger poised on the recorder. They stayed in the basement for an hour, going over the routine six times. Eric put the recorder on automatic then, to be activated only if there were a sound. He connected a warning buzzer to be sounded in the house above if the recorder came on, and they left. Tippy was scowling in discouragement.

"Remember that we agreed that it would be pretty stupid if it came out at the first indication of awareness," Eric said.

"I know," she said. "But why should it come out? It knows that it's perfectly safe in its little hiding place, probably just waiting to attack again. I think we should burn down the house and forget the whole thing."

Eric nodded at her. If the thing was listening to them with any understanding, it would know that they were aware of it now, and that they could drive it out to the open with fire. Now they would wait and see.

The Groth listened and understood the reasoning behind the statement. They were familiar to it. It had learned the female already, and knew that she could not be used for its purpose. It would learn the male later, when his guard was down. It withdrew from the female reluctantly; she was very nearly suitable, but there was a hindrance in her mind that would require many long hours of persistent training to overcome, and the Groth wouldn't have the time for that. She had spent years learning to think with a certain logic that Earthmen believed was necessary to education, and the training was of the sort that interfered with extrasensory abilities. It could be overcome, if her latent ability were powerful enough, but only with time. The Groth examined again the crude apparatus they had assembled in the lowest level of the building, and it knew they would try again to contact it. Suddenly the loneliness of the long years without the lifemate overwhelmed it, and it let its thoughts curl about the buzzer and the recorder. It could communicate again, ease the last years, perhaps enlist their help through explanations. . . . It withdrew from the equipment and listened again to the words being spoken above it.

"How I would have loved this house when I was a child," Tippy said.

They were going up the wide stairs side by side, talking. They separated at the top of the steps to get dressed for swimming. The Groth followed Tippy to her room and examined it through a tiny part of her mind without intruding to the point of being felt. If she were the other female, it thought, it wouldn't have been able to do even that much. The other female was too receptive. It wished the other female had come back instead of this one. It left her then and found the male again, but without entering his mind at all yet. It couldn't afford to drive them away again. There might not be another chance if they left.

It watched them play in the cold water of the lake, and again it felt the pang of loneliness, stabbing harder this time, taking longer to banish. It visualized the young of Gron also at play in the water. It wanted desperately to enter one of the minds and feel the water on skin, but it resisted the urge and watched from the outside until they reentered the house, shivering.

"You go shower and get something on and I'll make a fire," Eric said. "Then it'll be time to try the beast again."

"Be right down," Tippy said. When she returned, she had her hair wrapped in a towel. It was almost six.

"Drink?" Eric asked.

She shook her head. "Coffee, maybe." She went to the kitchen to make it, and Eric followed her.

"You don't seem at all alarmed by being here," he said.

"I know. It's that old, it-can't-happen-to-me syndrome." The coffee was starting to perk. "Let's go down and try it again now," she said.

The Groth watched and listened while they buzzed

and waited, and it wanted to answer them. As long as
they had been unaware of its presence, it had been
easy to think of them almost as animals, at least sub-
intelligent, but now they were suddenly communicat-
ing beings. And the Groth was lonely.

"It isn't going to answer us, is it?" Tippy said, in the
living room again. She was brushing her hair, drying it
before the fire.

"I don't know."

"It isn't. Let's not go to the restaurant like we
planned. I'll make us something here." She kept her
gaze on the flickering fire. Eric stared at her for
several moments before he answered.

"We promised each other that we would stick to
the plan we made," he said slowly. "That was one of
the conditions, remember?"

"I know, but— Look, it took us days to make up our
minds to try this. Why should we expect it to make
up its mind within minutes or even hours, to answer
our signal? I hadn't thought of that until now. We
have to give it a chance."

Eric lit a cigarette and studied it intently. "Have you
felt anything at all?"

"Nothing. Unless just a little bit foolish."

He grinned at that. "Yeah. I know. Okay, we'll eat
in. But the rest of the plan stays unchanged. No arguing about the motel later. Okay?"

"Sure."

The Groth continued to listen to them, and it came
to understand that they were going away again later.
It sank down in the tank thinking furiously. They
couldn't leave now. It could communicate with them
and possibly hold them that way. But they might have
planned to call in authorities if it made such a move.
It would have to probe to learn what their plans actually were. It sighed.

Tippy talked as she prepared their dinner, and once
when she looked up from the pot she was stirring,

she caught Eric's gaze on her in a look that made her stop completely. She turned back to the stove in confusion.

"It's okay," Eric said, as she stirred vigorously. "Relax."

"I don't know what you mean."

"You know exactly what I mean. And you're stirring gravy out all over the stove."

She moved the pan. "It's not gravy. It's spaghetti sauce. You're too old for me." She looked him up and down. "You're my father's partner."

Eric laughed. "If you haven't burned the sauce completely, let's eat."

She laughed too then, and knew that he wasn't too old at all.

The Groth continued to watch them as they chatted and relaxed. The male was the one to probe for the plans they had made. He would not alarm as easily as the female, who had felt the probe once before. It waited until they were again comfortable before the fire, and it began to send peaceful rhythms and harmonies at them, such as were used for the Groth young. The male became wary and uneasy. The Groth withdrew. They had used sequence in their abortive attempt to contact it; perhaps sequence would quiet them. It sent a slower cadence at them, and this was useful. The male relaxed again. When the Groth touched his mind, however, the male stiffened and sent hate and panic thoughts, and the rational mind was totally submerged. The Groth withdrew hurriedly before it was damaged again by the emotions of the Earthpeople.

"Eric! Are you all right? What happened?" Tippy shook him hard.

"It's gone now, I think. I . . . I guess I know what you felt before." Eric felt shaken and curiously ashamed. His reaction had been so uncontrolled; the hatred that had poured over him left him shaken. "It's here," he said. His voice was too tight and flat. "And we've got to find it and destroy it. A thing like that can't go on living in the same world with men and women. It's pure evil."

Tippy stared at him. "Let's go," she said. "It . . . it killed Dwight, and almost killed Mother. I don't know why we thought we could— Let's go!"

Her voice rose and Eric nodded.

The Groth couldn't let them leave. It was still shuddering from the emotional shock of the male's mind, but it knew that if they left now, there would be no future hope in time to save the mission. Its only hope for personal survival as well as the success of its mission was to get into space beyond the reach of Earthmen and go into suspended animation and await the Gron ship. It had to have their help. It reached out for the male. They were in the back of the building, near the outside door. It touched the male very easily, trying to do little damage and still hold him. The male fell down. The Groth knew that he was not dead, but in a deep trancelike state from which he would not awaken for hours. The female was screaming hysterically. She was not moving, simply screaming. The Groth retreated from her unvoiced screams: she was calling her mother and father. Not using her voice, not even knowing that she was calling them, she was screaming over and over for her mother and father. Then for her mother only. The Groth tried to be even more gentle with her than it had been with the male, but she too fell unconscious to the floor. The Groth felt its strength ebbing, and knew that again the contact had hurt it. It sank down into its tank. It was excreting alarmingly. It needed time to rest. The male and female would not stir now, and the Groth could rest. It let its mind go slack, and the too accessible dreams came and lulled it to sleep.

Mandy sat straight up, a questioning look on her face. Tippy? She started for the apartment door, then stopped in confusion. She heard it again. Or felt it.

Tippy! But where? Robert coughed in the other room, and she turned to go to him, to ask if he heard, but again she stopped. She was shaking hard suddenly, and her legs were weak; she almost fell before she got back to her chair. Was she really having a breakdown then? Voices in her head. A thrill of fear stirred in her loins, and vividly she recalled another time that she had heard Tippy's voice in her head. She had run out the door in time to jump into the front seat of the rolling car and put her foot on the brake before it had rolled backward off the road and over a cliff. Tippy was sitting without motion or sound on the front seat, four years old, terrified at what she had done. It was the same feeling now.

Where are you? she cried silently, and there was no answer. Nothing was there now, but her own fear. Slowly, still unsteady, she rose and started toward the door. She looked back at the bedroom door, but didn't tell Robert anything. He was reading in bed, would fall asleep soon, never realize that she was out. If she told him, he would try to stop her; he would stop her. She bit her lip hard and blinked back the tears that had come to her eyes. But it wasn't his fault. He simply couldn't stand things that didn't have explanations, and this didn't. She had to go out. She didn't know where she was going, but she had to get started.

She got the car from the building parking lot and started up the West Side Drive, still with no destination. She drove steadily and when she crossed the Tappan Zee Bridge, it was as if she had known from the start that she was going to the house. She didn't pause when the realization struck her.

She was not surprised to see the house lighted, with Eric's car in the driveway. She went to the kitchen door as if drawn there, and was not surprised to see the couple sprawled on the floor. She knelt by Tippy and felt her pulse, then Eric's. They were both unconscious only. She was starting for the telephone when she felt it.

The Groth woke with a start, chagrined to find that it had been dozing. The other female was there. The Groth had learned the way into her, but it hesitated, knowing that it had to use great caution, afraid that she would go into shock again at its touch. It used a probe that was as gentle and loving as the exploratory probe of a lifemate in its first contact.

Mandy moaned and clutched her head, swaying. Please, she whimpered, not again. Please. The fire spread and she began to weep. The Groth was swept by anguish waves that loosened its control momentarily, and it got the force of her fear like a battering ram against its own brain. It concentrated on symbols that she could understand and found the intelligent part of her brain out of reach, dominated by the savage, uncontrollable sub-brain. It was like fighting a horde of demons that swirled out of focus to merge with one another and assume shapes even more frightening. She had closed her eyes tight at the first touch, but suddenly she opened them wide, and the Groth shrank back from the glare of the room where she was. She was sobbing and calling to it to go away. The Groth knew then that it had to take full control, whether or not she was damaged. Deep in the vlen the Groth closed its eyes against the pain of too bright light, and Mandy's eyes closed also. It willed its breathing to become slower and more regular, and her sobbing eased. The Groth knew that she would have to use its suit to withstand the sulphur atmosphere in the ship. She would need oxygen also, but that would be found at the lake. This was not what it had wanted. This was a criminal act. There was no cooperation, but simply control.

Slowly, like a sleepwalker, Mandy started for the basement steps. She was still clutching her bag. She crossed the basement and waited until she was taken inside the wine cellar to find a garment there. She dropped the bag when she picked up the suit, and she turned and retraced her steps up and out of the house to her car. Her keys were still in the ignition. Her hand reached for the key, and she opened her eyes wide and started to tremble. The horror in her mind penetrated her understanding a little; she screamed and looked about wildly. Then it was back, the burning, crawling thing in her brain was there again. The look of near comprehension was replaced by the blankness of a somnambule, and she turned on the ignition and backed to make her turn and leave.

The Groth's body went hot with the realization that it had nearly lost her. It shivered in the tank and forced concentration back in full force. If only it hadn't been so weakened by injuries and the destructive invasions of its mind by the eroding hatred of the Earthpeople. . . . It had tried to find out from her the location of the lake, going to it by road, and in doing so, it had loosened its grip on the hind brain that was now guiding her every action. It had to rely on her own knowledge to get her there, hoping that she knew the way without direction. If only it could deal directly with her rational mind, but in the Earthmen, the rational mind was forever in danger of being eclipsed by the irrational hind brain that allowed no hope of intelligent behavior. The Groth strained to maintain the contact as distance separated it from the female, and with each mile, the difficulty increased. It was totally unaware of the stirring of the male in the building above it.

Eric felt as though its head were split wide open. He opened his eyes warily and concentrated on puzzling out what the strange noise was that he was hearing. Then he remembered. He sat up too fast and was punished by a stab of pain. Tippy! She stirred and moaned at his touch, and only then did he realize he was hearing the buzzer they had rigged to the recorder in the basement.

"Tippy, snap out of it! Come on. You're okay. It's gone now."

She opened her eyes and panic came through until

she saw Eric bending over her. She looked past him, then searched the rest of the kitchen in a quick glance. "What— The alarm! It's out!"

"I don't know what the hell's been going on," Eric said. He hauled her to her feet and pushed her toward the door. "Go get in the car and start it. I'm going to take a quick look in the basement."

Tippy drew back and held his arm. "Not alone," she said. "Let me stay with you."

Eric scowled, but together they went to the small entry at the back door and stared at the basement door standing open.

"I closed it," he said softly. "I remember that I closed it." They stared down the stairs and finally he said, "Oh, hell. I'm going to get the recorder and bring it up to see what we got. That fool buzzer is driving me out of my mind."

The buzzer stopped abruptly when he grabbed the recorder from the bench and ran back to the stairs. "The door to the wine cellar is open," he said as he rewound the tape to the start position. He turned it to play and they listened. There was a creaking noise, a soft thud of something falling, then nothing for a long time. Eric turned it faster so that the tape spun through, but still nothing was on it until pounding steps came through and the silence of having the recorder stopped.

Tippy stared at it in bewilderment. "Once more," she said. When the creaking finished she stopped the recorder. "That's the door to the wine cellar. It sticks every time. Something came out . . ."

"Or went in."

"Then the thud." She started it again and stopped it when the dropping noise played. "What. . . We'll have to go down to find out, won't we?"

They went down and crossed the floor to the wine cellar. Tippy screamed when she saw what had made the thud.

"It's Mother's bag! It took her inside with it!"

Eric got Tippy back up to the kitchen, then called Robert. To Tippy he said, "He's looking around for her. She didn't say anything about leaving." He listened again, then said slowly, "You'd better get out to the house. Mandy's been here, but there's no car here now." He agreed to call the state police and hung up.

The troopers put out an alert for Mandy's car, and then started another search of the house, as fruitless as their previous search had been. The Groth became aware of the probing in the wine cellar, and Mandy almost skidded off the road. It turned its full attention to her again. Mandy was driving well, but too fast. She slowed down. Each moment for her was sufficient to itself; there was no future, no past. It was exactly like a dream in which anything can be accepted no matter how unrelated it is to anything else. She performed well, obeyed traffic laws, was careful at intersections, and had no thought about where she was going, or why. She was driving, and that was enough. Now and again there was a flash of terror and repulsion, but always it was banished very quickly, and she no longer was aware of any physical discomfort. The Groth was delighted with the facilitation that had been accomplished so quickly. It knew that the experiences it had shared with her before had made this contact possible, and it wasn't deceived into thinking it could yet communicate with her rational mind directly. Trying that would set up such an inner conflict within her that she probably would be lost to it. It listened briefly to the searchers, and now there was added a new silent voice calling her, through the Groth, reaching for her. It tried to shut out the mental cries and succeeded only partially. It felt the impact on the female and redoubled its efforts to keep her under control.

She drove north on secondary roads until she turned to a narrow blacktop road that led to the south shore of the lake.

The Groth felt the agonized call again and again, and it knew it had to still the silent voice bombarding its brain. Mandy's car swerved and braked hard. "No!" she screamed, aloud and in her mind. She pulled away from the Groth, and there was a meaningless jumble where there had been order in her mind. She had understood its thought! The Groth brought her back, but not fully yet, and both felt the struggle as she fought to stay free. She was nearly hysterical with her effort, and the Groth was excreting so dangerously that it feared unconsciousness would end the battle. The Groth understood that it was her lifemate who was calling to her through it, and it knew that it could not harm the lifemate and still keep the female under control. With the understanding that reached the Groth, the female became compliant again and resumed the drive toward the lake.

Mandy saw the black water before her and turned left. That was the way. She would need diving gear. That she had never dived before didn't occur to her then. She would need a tank of oxygen in order to clear the door and attach the air lock, and to breathe after she had got inside the ship. She stopped the car shortly after turning, and she parked it carefully in brush so that it couldn't be seen from the road. Then she pulled the garment from the car, and found the bubble air lock rolled up inside it. The Groth worked hard to reach out with her mind to find the oxygen, and twice while it searched, it almost lost contact with the female. Each time the primal fears rose in her; each time there was a battle again for control. The Groth knew that it was weakening rapidly. It had to finish soon, or it would lose after all. If only the pounding from the building would cease, and it didn't refer then to the physical search that was continuing. Robert was beating it down, and it would do nothing about the male adult. It had touched him once only, and it had found an infirmity that could bring about death almost instantly if the provocation were great enough. Probing by the Groth would be great enough. It located oxygen tanks finally, and again Mandy was moving with purpose. She stole a tank from a cabin, walking within feet of the slumbering occupants and out again, back to the lake. The Groth understood the principle of the tanks, but it had not used anything like them, and it was a matter of trial and error until the tank was strapped to Mandy's back. She had donned the garment without hesitation when directed to do so, and now with the tank in place, she was ready. That the suit was two feet too long for her didn't matter; she would have no real swimming to do. And her fingers could work, even though most of the digit holes had been left empty. She walked out awkwardly into the water, breathing uncertainly through the mouthpiece, but showing no fear of submerging. The Groth felt very proud of her, and she seemed to be aware of its pleasure. It felt that there was less resistance to it. But there was none of the real joy lifemates knew when they were working in harmony.

The Earthmen in the building housing the vlen had a digging machine at work. The Groth had to explore it, to assess its threat. They were going through the earth cellar, would strike the compressed soil that surrounded the vlen within an hour. It would stop them, of course, but if they decided to blast it with explosives, then they would know that it wasn't merely rock they were hitting. . . . But all that would take time, and perhaps by the time they got that far, it would be far out in space . . .

Mandy sank to the bottom of the lake, fighting for air, thrashing her arms and legs in a futile attempt to swim. She was being held down by the winding material that covered her completely, and stank, and there was no air. She clutched at the material over her face and tried to rip it away. Her lungs were bursting, and a curious lightheadedness overcame her. Her thrashing motions were weaker. The pain in her lungs and fear were all she knew, and abruptly it was back with her.

Help me, she begged it. Help me. Please.

There was no fight this time. It directed her hands to the air hose and got it in place. She choked on the first breath of air, and it soothed her and quieted her so that she could breathe normally. It wondered at the tears from its own eyes. It couldn't leave her again. If she did that inside the ship, she would die almost instantly, and her death would be ugly. It fastened all its resources on her then, and she got the air lock in place and went inside it. She turned on the tiny pump, and when the water was exhausted, she opened the door to the ship and entered that. The Groth saw it with its own eyes, and with hers, and it was shocked by the difference. She thought it was hideous, all dark and fungilike with strange shapes that faded from sight in shadows. It took her to the controls and checked them out. . . . Why didn't someone do something to quiet that male, her lifemate? It tried to close him out, but the lifemate was getting stronger, harder to keep away. She felt his call too, and symbols unfamiliar to the Groth rose and had to be quieted again. It made her work fast, but her hands were clumsy in the suit that was not designed for creatures with only five short fingers. It wondered how they had come down from the trees with such hands. The Groth thought gloomily that it might have to abandon the ship, the vlen, the data bank in orbit, everything.

Then the ship stirred slowly away from the muck at the bottom of the lake. The Groth searched through her for observers and found the area clear, and only then pushed the control that took the ship aloft. The ship went straight up as her hands waited for it to do something else with them. The Groth realized how much flying depended on conditioned reflex, how little on conscious control. It had to think hard to keep her eyes turned in the right direction so that it could see the controls. It felt so different now to do with its mind what its fingers had done without its conscious attention. It leveled off much too high, and there was not complete contact.

Mandy stared in horror at the controls before her eyes. She knew that she mustn't let go of the air hose again, and she clamped her teeth hard on the mouthpiece when she felt a scream welling up. Not now. Where was the creature? Where was she? She didn't dare move her hands. Somehow she found it, or it found her, and despite all her terror at finding herself alone in the ship, she found herself fighting it again, trying to push it away, shrinking from the repulsive, creeping, burning probe that curled through her brain.

The Groth knew it was being too harsh with her this time. It felt it in the slump of her body, which would have fallen to the floor of the ship without its support. It had entered her again without the gentle, subtle approach, thinking that by now she should be accustomed to it. She wasn't. Never would be, it appeared. Her body responded to its commands, but there was no time now to be easy on her. The ship was turned and homed in on the vlen and the tunnel entrance. It hovered over the area and descended softly to the clearing near the boulder that concealed the entrance. The female turned the ship in the right direction and turned on the energy beam that made moving the boulder a matter of directing it only. The energy flowed into the tunnel, and at the far end of it, the Groth started the computer on its way out. The beam carried it along effortlessly, drew it up into the ship. One by one the Groth's furnishings were drawn aboard, and suddenly the female broke loose. She was standing on the ground, close to the ship.

"Robert!" she screamed. She looked about her at the strange ship, and felt the burn of the acidic air, and opened her mouth to scream again. The Groth touched her, and when she fell, it moved her carefully to where she would be able to breathe her own air. It made certain that she was alive, but it was hard to be certain that she would stay alive. It hurried and finished cleaning out the vlen. The male lifemate was leaving the building. The Groth followed him with part of its mind, and it brought the walls of the vlen inward with the remaining instruments it had with it. It backed out of the tunnel, collapsing the walls as it went. Outside, it replaced the boulder. It stopped and looked down at the female lying on the ground, and very carefully it probed her again. She moaned. The Groth examined the extent of the acid burns she had suffered, and found that they were negligible; she was in shock now. Using great care, it had her remove the suit she wore. Then it soothed her mind, giving her the image of the Gron sea with cool, dim lights playing on the surface, and gentle swells lulling one into deep, healing sleep. It gave her the feeling of love and peace that went with the image. Her breathing became less labored, and her heart became regular and stronger. It could do no more for her. The lifemate was coming toward them fast now, homing in on her with a steadfastness that was unbelievable in one so lacking in training. The Groth climbed inside the ship and took a deep breath of fresh air there. It left the spot before Robert arrived, climbing straight up and away from Earth, a dark shadow without sound. It was so tired that it didn't know if it would recover from this ordeal or not. But that was a small matter. The mission would be successful. The Groth would be able to study the Earthmen and when time for contact came, it would be made with a minimum of strain, and a maximum of good will. That was the important thing.

Mandy woke up screaming, and continued to scream until there was a jab of a needle in her arm. When she woke again, Robert was beside her, but the room was painfully bright. She shut her eyes hard, almost remembering . . . something. It was gone. She was in a hospital room; she knew the smell of it, the texture of the sheets on the bed, the distant sounds that went with a hospital.

"You're all right, Mandy," Robert said. There was an anxious tone in his voice that said he wasn't certain that she was though. She opened her eyes again and the strangeness gave way slowly to familiarity. Robert was gray with black circles under his eyes.

"Did you see . . . anything?" she asked. Her mouth and throat hurt.

"There wasn't anything there to see. You have to believe that, Mandy. You have to. We tore the basement apart, searched every inch of the woods, called in experts. Nothing was there!"

"Tippy? Eric?"

"They're fine. Mandy, they won't let me stay long with you. Please try to understand that nothing was there. Eric must have fallen and hit his head. Tippy panicked when she saw him on the floor. She fainted. We questioned them a dozen times and neither of them knows anything at all. After we finished with the basement, even Eric had to admit that nothing could have been down there. Mandy, look at me. You do believe me, don't you?"

She closed her eyes slowly, this time in weariness. There was something just on the edge of awareness, if only she could turn quickly enough she would be able to see it. "Why did you go into the woods? You found me, didn't you?"

"I don't know. I must have heard you scream. I can't remember now, but it must have been a noise you made."

In quick succession she caught snatches of scenes: a lake, black with night, going into it; a ship of some sort; a strange creature that was hurt and lonely and terrifying and repellent. And lovely. She tried to hold onto one of the images, but couldn't. She couldn't connect them with anything.

"How did you get burned, Mandy? Do you remember?" Robert asked.

She shook her head, not opening her eyes. But it was there, too, fading away out of reach. If only he could see with her, help her understand. What little she did retain he would reject. There was no proof, no way to demonstrate it, to weigh it, measure it, compare it to other experiences. Her thoughts were becoming distorted as she drifted back toward sleep and she cried out. Robert squeezed her hand, and she never had felt so alone in her life. Where she was hurt and afraid, he couldn't reach. Then there was something else there, an image of a cool, dimly lighted sea where young played and gentle swells lulled one to deep, peaceful sleep, and where one had love and peace, and was never alone. She smiled and fell asleep again. After a moment Robert released her hand.

"There wasn't anything there," he said under his breath, looking down at her. "We would have found a trace of something." But where had she been? What had happened to her? What was causing her to smile so tenderly in her sleep now? Dully he left the room. They would call him when she woke up again. He walked silently down the empty hospital corridor to the room they had given him for the night, and he knew that the walls and doors didn't matter at all. He was no more separated from her by them than he was when he stood at her side and held her hand and failed to share what she felt, what she thought, what memories caused her first to cry out in terror, then to smile in her sleep. No matter how close they were, they were so far apart, so alone. Always so alone.

ABOUT THE AUTHOR

KATE WILHELM is the author of numerous books of provocative fiction, including *Abyss, The Downstairs Room, More Bitter Than Death, The Nevermore Affair,* and *Margaret and I.* Her short story "The Planners" won the Nebula Award in 1968. She lives with her husband, writer Damon Knight, and her children in Madeira Beach, Florida.

OUT OF THIS WORLD!

That's the only way to describe Bantam's great series of science-fiction classics. These space-age thrillers are filled with terror, fancy and adventure and written by America's most renowned writers of science fiction. Welcome to outer space and have a good trip!

☐	THE TIME MACHINE by H. G. Wells	4063	50¢
☐	A CANTICLE FOR LEIBOWITZ by Walter Miller, Jr.	5423	95¢
☐	THE MYSTERIOUS ISLAND by Jules Verne	5439	75¢
☐	THE DAY OF THE DRONES by A. M. Lightner	5567	75¢
☐	THE MARTIAN CHRONICLES by Ray Bradbury	5613	95¢
☐	20,000 LEAGUES UNDER THE SEA by Jules Verne	5939	75¢
☐	ALAS, BABYLON by Pat Frank	6991	95¢
☐	FANTASTIC VOYAGE by Isaac Asimov	7137	95¢
☐	RAGA SIX by Frank Lauria	7249	$1.25
☐	STAR TREK I by James Blish	7869	75¢